PRAISE FOR DIANA PALMER

"Nobody tops Diana Palmer
when it comes to delivering pure,
undiluted romance. I love her stories."
—*New York Times* bestselling author Jayne Ann Krentz

"Diana Palmer is a mesmerizing storyteller who
captures the essence of what a romance should be."
—*Affaire de Coeur*

"Diana Palmer is a unique talent
in the romance industry. Her writing
combines wit, humor, and sensuality;
and, as the song says, nobody does it better!"
—*New York Times* bestselling author Linda Howard

"No one beats this author for sensual anticipation."
—*Rave Reviews*

"A love story that is pure and enjoyable."
—*Romantic Times* on *Lord of the Desert*

"The dialogue is charming, the characters
likeable and the sex sizzling..."
—*Publishers Weekly* on *Once in Paris*

Diana Palmer has published over seventy category romances, as well as historical romances and longer contemporary works. With over forty million copies of her books in print, *New York Times* bestselling author Diana Palmer is one of North America's most beloved authors. Her accolades include seven national Waldenbooks bestseller awards, four national B. Dalton bestseller awards, two Bookrak national sales awards, a Lifetime Achievement Award for series storytelling from *Romantic Times* magazine, several *Affaire de Coeur* awards and two regional RWA awards. Diana resides in the north mountains of her home state of Georgia with her husband, James, and their son, Blayne Edward.

DIANA PALMER

If Winter Comes

Published by Silhouette Books
America's Publisher of Contemporary Romance

SILHOUETTE BOOKS

ISBN 0-373-51278-3

IF WINTER COMES

First published in North America as a MacFadden Romance by Kim Publishing Corporation.

One

It was an election morning in the newsroom, and Carla Maxwell felt the excitement running through her slender body like a stab of lightning. The city hall beat which she shared with Bill Peck was a dream of a job. Something was always happening—like this special election to fill a vacant seat created by a commissioner's resignation. There were only five men on the city commission, and this was the Public Works seat. Besides that, the two men running for it were, respectively, a good friend and a deadly foe of the present mayor, Bryan Moreland.

"How does it look?" Carla called to Peck, who was impatiently running a hand through his gray-streaked blond hair as he hung onto a telephone receiver waiting for the results from the city's largest precinct.

"Neck and neck, to use a trite expression." He grinned at her. He had a nice face, she thought. Lean and smooth and kind. Not at all the usual expressionless mask worn by most veteran newsmen.

She smiled back, and her dark green eyes caught the light and seemed to glow under the fluorescent lights.

"What precinct are you waiting for?" Beverly Miller, the Society Editor, asked, pausing by Peck's desk.

"Ward four," he told her. "It looks

like…hello? Yes, go ahead.'' He scribbled feverishly on his pad, thanked his caller and hung up. He shook his head. ''Tom Green took the fourth by a small avalanche,'' he said, leaning back in his chair. ''Now there's a surprise for you. A political novice winning a city election in a three-man field with no run-off.''

''I'll bet Moreland's tickled to death,'' Carla said dryly. ''Green's been at his throat ever since he took office almost four years ago.''

''He may not run again now,'' Beverly laughed. ''He hasn't announced.''

''He will,'' Peck said confidently. ''Moreland's one hell of a fighter.''

''That's the truth,'' Beverly said, perching her ample figure on the edge of Peck's desk. She smiled at Carla. ''You haven't been here long enough to know much of Moreland's background, but he started out as one of the best trial lawyers in the city. He had a national reputation long before he ran for mayor and won. And despite agitators like Green, he commands enough public respect to keep the office if he wants it. He's done more for urban renewal, downtown improvement and city services than any mayor in the past two decades."

"Then why do we keep hearing rumors of graft?" Carla asked Peck when Beverly was called away to her phone.

"What rumors?" Peck asked, even as he began feeding his copy into the electronic typewriter.

"I've had two anonymous phone calls this week," she told him, pushing a strand of dark hair back under the braided coil pinned on top her head. "Big Jim gave me the green light to do some investigating."

"Where do you plan to start?" he asked indulgently.

"At the city treasury. One particular department was singled out by my anonymous friend," she added. "I was told that if I checked the books, I'd find some very interesting entries."

"Tell me what you're looking for, and I'll check into it for you," he volunteered.

She cocked her head at him. "Thanks—" she smiled "—but no thanks. Just because I'm fresh out of college, don't think I need a shepherd. My father owned a weekly paper in south Georgia."

"No wonder you feel so comfortable here," he chuckled. "But remember that a weekly and a daily are worlds apart."

"Don't be arrogant," she chided. "If you tried to hire on at a weekly, you'd very likely find that your experience wouldn't be enough."

"Oh?"

"You have one beat," she reminded him. "City Hall. You don't cover fashion shows or go to education board meetings, or cover the county morgue. Those are other beats. But,'' she added, ''on a weekly you're responsible for news, period. The smaller the weekly, the smaller the staff, the more responsibility you have. I worked for Dad during the summers. I was my own editor, my own proofreader, my own photographer, and I had to get all the news all the time. Plus that, I had to help set the copy if Trudy got sick, I had to do layout and paste-up and write ads, and set headlines, and sell ads...''

''I surrender!'' Peck laughed. ''I'll just stick to this incredibly easy job I've got, thanks.''

''After seventeen years, I'm not surprised.''

He raised a pale eyebrow at her, but he didn't make another comment.

Later, as they were on their way out of the building, Peck groaned while he scanned the front page of the last edition.

"God help us, that's not what he said!" he burst out.

"Not what who said?" She pushed through the door onto the busy sidewalk and waited for him.

"Moreland. The paper says he stated that the city would pick up the tab for new offices at city hall...." Peck ran a rough hand through his hair. "I told that damned copy editor twice that Moreland said he *wouldn't* agree to redecorate city hall! Oh, God, he'll eat us alive tonight."

Tonight was when one of the presidential advisers was speaking at a local civic organization's annual meeting, to which she and Peck were invited. It would be followed by a reception at a local state legislator's home, and Moreland would certainly be there.

"I'll wear a blond wig and a mustache," she assured him. "And you can borrow one of my dresses."

His pale eyes skimmed over her tall, slender body appreciatively, before he considered his own compact, but husky physique. "I'd need a bigger size, but thanks for the thought."

"Maybe he won't blame us," she said comfortingly.

"We work for the paper," he reminded her. "And the fact that a story I called in got fouled up won't cut any ice. Don't sweat it, honey, it's my fault not yours. Moreland doesn't eat babies."

"I'm twenty-three, you know," she said with a smile. "I was late getting into college."

"Moreland's older than I am," he persisted. "He's got to be pushing forty, if he isn't already there."

"I know, I've seen the gray hairs."

"Most of those he got from the accident," he murmured as they got to the parking lot. "Tragic thing, and so senseless. Didn't even scratch the other driver. I guess the other guy was too drunk to notice any injuries, even if he had them."

"That was before my time," she said. She paused at the door of her yellow Volkswagen. "Was it since he was elected?"

"Two years ago." He nodded. "There were rumors of a split between him and his wife, but no confirmation."

"Any kids?"

"A daughter, eight years old."

She nodded. "She must be a comfort to him."

"Honey, she was in the car," he told her. "He was the only survivor."

She swallowed hard. "He doesn't look as if bullets would scratch him. I guess after that, they wouldn't."

"That's what I hear." He opened the door of his car. "Need a ride to the meeting?"

She shook her head. "Thanks, any-way. I thought I might toss my clothes in the trunk and stop by a laundromat after the reception."

He froze with his hand on the door handle. "Wash clothes at a laundromat at midnight in an evening gown?"

"I'm going to wear a dress, not an evening gown, and the laundromat be-longs to my aunt and uncle. They'll be there."

He let out a deep breath. "Don't scare me like that. It's not good for a man of my advanced years."

"What a shame, and I was going to buy you a racing set for Christmas, too."

"Christmas is three months away."

"Is that all?" she exclaimed. "Well, maybe I'd better forego the meeting and go Christmas shopping instead."

"And leave me to face Moreland alone?" He looked deserted, tragic.

"I can't protect you. He towers over

me, you know,'' she added, remembering the sheer physical impact of the man at the last city commission meeting.

"He's never jumped on you,'' he reminded her. He smiled boyishly. "In fact, at that last budget meeting we covered, he seemed to spend a lot of time looking at you.''

Her eyebrows went up. "At me? I wonder what I did?''

He shook his head. "Carla, you're without hope. Men do look at attractive women.''

"Not men like Moreland,'' she protested.

"Men like Moreland,'' he insisted. "He may be the mayor, honey, but he's still very much a man.''

"He could have almost any socialite in the city.''

"But he rarely dates,'' he said. "I've seen him with a woman twice at a couple of social functions. He's not what you'd call a womanizer, unless he's keeping a very low profile."

"Maybe he misses his wife," she said softly.

"Angelica wasn't the kind of woman any sane man misses," he recalled with a smile. "She reminded me of a feisty dog—all snap and bristle. I think it was an arranged marriage rather than a love match. They were descended from two of the city's founding families, you know. Moreland could get along very well without working at all. He does it for a hobby, I think, although he takes it seriously. He loves this city, and he's sure worked for it."

"I still wouldn't like to have him mad at me," she admitted with a smile. "It would be like having a bulldozer run over you."

"Ask me when the party's over," he moaned, "and I'll let you know."

"Wear your track shoes," she called as she got into her car and drove away.

* * *

Carla and Peck sat together with his date, a ravishing blonde who couldn't seem to take her eyes off him. She felt vaguely alone at functions like this gigantic dinner. It was comforting to be near someone she knew, even if she did feel like a third wheel. Reporting had overcome some of her basic shyness, but not a lot. She still cringed at gatherings.

Even now, chic in an emerald green velour dress that was perfect with her pale green eyes and dark hair—which she wore, uncharacteristically, loose tonight—she felt self-conscious, especially when she caught Bryan Moreland's dark eyes looking at her from the head table. It was unnerving, that pointed stare of his, and she had a feeling that there was animosity in it. Perhaps he was blaming her as well as Peck for the story in the paper. She was Peck's protegee, after all, his shadow on the city hall beat while she was getting her bearings in the new environment of big-city journalism.

"His Honor's glaring at me," she told Peck over her coffee cup.

"Ignore him," he told her. "He glares at all reporters. See old Graham over at the next table—the *Sun* reporter?" he asked, gesturing toward a young, sandy-haired man with a photographer sitting next to him. "He axed the mayor's new landfill proposal without giving the city's side of the question. Moreland cornered him at a civic-club banquet and burned his ears off. In short," he concluded with a smile, "he would like to see you and me and Graham on the menu tonight—preferably served with barbeque sauce and apples in our mouths."

She shuddered. "How distasteful."

He nodded. "I'd sure give him indigestion, wouldn't I, lovely?" he asked the blonde, who smiled back.

"Never mind," Carla told her com-

panionably, "we'll flatter him by pretending we don't think he's a tough old
bird."

"Don't listen, Blanche," Peck told
the blonde.

The blonde winked at Carla. "Okay,
sugar, I won't."

When they finished the lavish meal,
the tall young presidential adviser, Joel
Blackwell, took the podium and Peck
and Carla produced pads and pens. It
had been Peck's idea to let Carla cover
meetings such as this, to give her a feel
for it, but he took his own notes as well,
as a backup, and wrote his own copy to
compare with hers. She was proving to
be an apt pupil, too. He was grudging
with his praise, but she was beginning
to earn her share of it.

Most of the speech was routine prop-
aganda for the administration: pinpoint-
ing the President's interest in his fan
mail and highlighting some less known
aspects of his personal life. When he

finished, he threw the floor open for questions, and foremost on the audience's mind was foreign relations. Domestic problems had a brief voice, followed by some questions on what a presidential adviser's duties consisted of. Carla took notes feverishly, blissfully unaware of Peck's indulgent smile as he jotted down a brief note here and there.

Finally, it was over, and the guests were gathering jackets and purses for a quick exit. Carla threw her lacy shawl around her shoulders and stood up.

"Well, I'll see you at the cocktail party," she told Peck and his girl friend. "I wish it were informal. My feet hurt!"

He gave her tight sandals with their high, spiked heels a distasteful glance. "No wonder." He caught Blanche by the arm, and drew her along through the crowd. "In the office, she kicks off her shoes and walks around barefoot on the carpet,'' he whispered conspiratorially.

"Can I help it if I'm a country girl at heart?'' Carla laughed. "I'm still adjusting to big-city life.''

"You'll get used to it,'' Peck promised her.

She sighed, smothering in perfume and cologne and the crush of people. "Oh, I hope so,'' she said under her breath.

Two

The cocktail party was far more of an ordeal for Carla than the dinner had been. She stood by the long bar that featured every kind of intoxicating beverage known to man, plus ice and shakers and glasses, trying to look sophisticated and nonchalant. Around her, expensively dressed women wearing jewels Carla couldn't afford time payments on were discussing new plays and art exhibits, dripping diamonds and prestige. A tiny smile touched Carla's full mouth. How horrible, she thought wickedly, to be that rich and have to worry about having your diamonds stolen. Or to have a swimming pool and all the bother of getting leaves cleaned out of it every fall.

The mind boggles, she told herself as she idly glanced around the room. Ironically, the first person she recognized was the mayor.

Bryan Moreland was unmistakable, even with his broad back turned. Carla studied him from across the room, her dancing eyes curious. She'd seen the big man often enough on television, not to mention in the flesh, but every time she was around him he seemed to be bigger and broader and darker than he looked before.

His hair was dark, threaded with gray, and thick and straight. His complexion was very tanned, as if he spent a lot of time in the sun rather than in an office, and her eyes were drawn to the hand holding his cigarette—a darkly masculine hand with long fingers and a black onyx ring on the little finger. His suits looked as if they had to be tailor-made for him, because he was well over six feet tall. He had an athlete's build, and he moved like a cat, all rippling muscle and grace as he turned abruptly and strode toward the bar.

Carla started at the suddenness of the move. She almost stepped away, but she wasn't quick enough. He saw her, and since her face was one he knew, he headed straight for her.

His dark eyes narrowed as he stopped just a couple of feet away and glowered down at her, pinning her. She felt apprehension shiver through her frozen body before he spoke, and her hand tightened on the glass of cola she was drinking instead of liquor.

"That was one hell of a mistake in your morning edition," he said without preamble, his voice deep and slow and cutting. "My phone rang off the hook all day and I had to get on the damned evening news to get the noose off my neck."

"I'm sorry," she began automatically, "but it wasn't my..."

"The next time, check your facts with me before you run back and print some pack of lies!" he growled, his deep voice reverberating like thunder. "What the hell do you people do with news down there, make it up as you go along?"

She licked her lips nervously. She wasn't usually intimidated this easily. Being attacked went with the job, and most of the time she handled it well, diplomatically. But it wasn't easy to be diplomatic with a steamroller, and that was what Moreland brought to mind.

"It was the..." she began again.

"Why don't you go back to journalism school and learn how to verify information?" he growled. "My God, children are taking over the world!" His eyes narrowed dangerously. "I'll expect not only a retraction, but an apology."

"Mr. Moreland, I'm really sorry...." she whispered unsteadily, feeling about two inches high.

He poured himself a drink—Scotch, she noticed—with incredibly steady hands, his face like granite, and she wondered idly if anything ever rattled him. He would have made a fantastic racing driver or doctor, she thought suddenly, with those steady hands and nerves.

"I didn't go to Ed Hart this time," he said, tossing the publisher's name at her. He speared her with those demon eyes. "But if it ever happens again, I'll have your job."

He walked away without another

word, and she wanted to stand there and cry. The party had been ruined for her. Being blamed for a mistake was fine, if it was hers. But to get stuck with somebody else's, and not be given a chance to defend herself, now, that hurt.

She took a long sip of her drink and set it back on the bar, moving slowly, quietly, toward the ladies' room. Tears were welling in her eyes, and she didn't want the humiliation of shedding them in public.

She darted into the empty bathroom, locked the door, and leaned back against the wall, her eyes unseeing on the spacious, fully carpeted room with its lush champagne and gold decor. Tears ran silently down her cheeks. Why Moreland could affect her like that, she didn't know. But he seemed to have some inexplicable power to reduce her to the level of a wounded child.

She wiped at the tears with an impatient hand. This was ridiculous, she told herself. She couldn't afford to let people or things get to her like this. Hard knocks went with the job, and it was either get used to a little rough treatment or spend the rest of her life in tears. She'd have to toughen up. Her father had told her that at the beginning, the day she announced that she'd entered journalism school at the university.

She found a washcloth and tried to erase the telltale marks from her flushed young face. When she finished, her eyes were still red-rimmed, but all traces of tears were gone. She straightened her dress and ran a comb through her long, gently waving hair. Her pale green eyes surveyed the result coolly. It wasn't a pretty face, but her eyes were big and arresting, and her face had a softly vulnerable look about it.

She turned, adjusting the V-neckline of her dress with cold, nervous hands.

She'd rather have been shot than go through that door, but there was no way around it. Running away solved nothing. She'd learned that much, at least, in twenty-three years.

As she went back into the spacious living room, ironically, the first person she saw was Bryan Moreland. He stared over a shorter man's head at her, and his narrow dark eyes caught hers at once. She raised her chin proudly and gave him her best south Georgia glare.

Amazingly, as she watched, a slow, faint smile turned up his chiseled lips as if that silent show of rebellion amused him.

Carla turned, purse in hand, and made her way through the crowd to Bill Peck and Blanche.

Peck's eyes narrowed thoughtfully on her face. "He got you," he said immediately.

"Uncanny insight, Mr. Peck," she replied with a wan smile. "I didn't get the chance to plead my case. He must be absolute hell in a courtroom.''

''You'd think so if you'd ever seen him in one,'' the older reporter agreed. ''I've seen prospective witnesses cringe when they saw him coming. Was it rough?''

She shrugged, pretending a calm she didn't feel. ''A little skin's missing,'' she said with a laugh.

''Sorry,'' he said. ''That was my hiding you took.''

''The rewrite man's,'' she corrected. ''Don't worry about it. It goes with the job, remember? That's what everybody tells me.''

''Amen.''

''Well, I've gritted my teeth and made my appearance,'' she added. ''I've got my notes in my grubby little hand, and I'm getting out of here before His Honor takes another bite out of me. See you in the morning.''

''Don't brood on it,'' he cautioned.

"I won't." She smiled at the blonde. "Good night."

"Good night." Blanche smiled back. "Don't sweat it, honey, we all get our lumps occasionally, deserved or not."

"Sure," she said.

She wound her way through the crowd to Senator White and thanked him for the invitation, then she turned and moved quickly to the door. Just as her hand touched the doorknob, a large, warm hand covered it, effectively stopping her, and before she turned, she recognized the black onyx ring on the tanned, masculine hand.

"Peck told me what happened when you darted out of the room," Bryan Moreland said quietly, and she had to look up a long way to his face, despite her two-inch heels and her formidable five feet, seven inches of height. So that was why Bill had looked so unconcerned.

"Did he?" she asked wanly, meeting

the darkness in his eyes with uneasiness.

"I like to place blame where it's due," he said in his deep, lazy voice. "Why didn't you tell me you weren't responsible for that story?"

Her eyes flickered down to his burgundy tie. "You didn't give me much of a chance, Mr. Moreland," she said.

"Mister?" His heavy eyebrows went up. "God, do I look that old?"

"No, sir."

He sighed heavily. "Not going to forget it, are you?" he taunted.

She raised her eyes to his with a faint grin. "Not going to apologize, are you?" she returned.

Something kindled in his dark eyes, making them velvet soft, sensuous. A hint of a smile turned up a corner of his wide, firm mouth. She found herself blushing and hated the way she felt: young and gauche and very much outmatched.

"I haven't had much practice at it," he admitted.

"Always right, huh?" she asked.

"Cheeky little thing, aren't you?" he challenged.

"Nosey," she countered, and he chuckled deeply.

"Well, good night," she said, reaching again for the doorknob.

"Do you have a way home?" he asked unexpectedly.

All of a sudden, she wished with all her heart that she didn't. She somehow felt warm and soft inside, and she wanted to know more about the big man.

"Yes," she replied reluctantly.

"Good night, then." He turned and left her at the door with her sudden, nagging disappointment.

She got down to the street where her car was parked just in time to be confronted with two tall, menacing boys. There were streetlights around the senator's palatial home, but it was a little-traveled street, and there wasn't a soul in sight. Carla started toward her car with sheer bravado, mentally cursing herself for coming out here alone.

"Ain't she pretty," one of the boys called with a long whistle, his voice slurred as if he'd been drinking.

"A looker, all right," the other commented, and they moved quickly toward her.

She fumbled in her purse for her car key, frantically digging through makeup and pens and pads with fingers that trembled.

"Nice," the older of the boys said, smiling at her from an unshaven face. "Where you going, baby? Me and John feel like a little company."

She straightened jerkily, fighting to remember her brief class in karate, the right moves at the right time.

"I don't want company," she said quietly. "And if you don't go away and leave me alone, I'm going to scream, very loud, so that those people in the house come out here.''

''I'm scared,'' the one called John laughed drunkenly. ''God, I'm scared! You think the old senator's going to come down here and save you?''

''He might not,'' Bryan Moreland said from the shadows, ''but I'll be glad to oblige.''

''I ain't scared of you, either,'' the older boy said, moving forward to throw a midriff punch toward the big man.

Moreland hardly seemed to move, but the next minute, the boy was crumpled on the pavement. The big man looked at the one called John. ''You've got two choices. One is pick up this litter from the street and carry it home. You don't want to know what the second one is.''

John stared at him for a moment, as if measuring his youth and slenderness against the older man's experience and pure athletic strength. He bent and helped his winded companion to his feet and they moved on down the sidewalk as quickly as they could.

Carla slumped against the small Beetle, her eyes closed as her heart shook her with its wild pounding. "That was close," she murmured breathlessly, opening her eyes to find Moreland very close. "Thank you."

"My pleasure. Are you all right?"

She nodded. "Sheer stupidity. I forgot how deserted it is out here."

"You'll remember next time, won't you?"

"Oh, yes," she said with a smile. "You're very good with your fists. I didn't even see you move."

"I boxed for a while when I was younger," he said.

"I didn't know boxing was around on the Ark," she commented seriously.

He chuckled. "That's a hell of a way to say thank you."

"You're the one harping on your ancientness, not me," she told him. "I just do my job and catch hell from bad-tempered public officials."

"I'm not always bad-tempered."

"Really?" she said unconvincingly.

"Have dinner with me tomorrow, and I'll prove it."

She stared at him as if she'd just been hit between the eyes with a block of ice. "What?"

"Have dinner with me. I'll take you disco dancing."

"You're the mayor!" she burst out.

"Well, my God, it didn't de-sex me," he replied.

She blushed. "I didn't mean it that way. It's just..."

"You can't maintain your objectivity, is that it? Honey, I don't mix politics and pleasure," he said quietly, "and right now I don't give a damn about your objectivity."

She felt the same way. Something strange and exciting was happening to her. Something she felt that he shared. It was almost frightening.

"I...I was going to do a series of articles on city officials," she said, seizing on a chance to do some quiet investigating about the information in her anonymous phone calls. "I could start with you...if you wouldn't mind," she added.

He pulled a package of cigarettes out of his pocket and offered her one, lifting an eyebrow when she refused. He lit one and repocketed his lighter, smoking quietly while he studied her from his superior height.

"How deep into my life do you want to delve?" he asked finally, and she knew he was thinking about the accident.

"Into your *political* life," she corrected. "I think privacy is a divine right as far as anyone's personal life is concerned. I wouldn't like mine in print."

"Oh?" His dark eyes sketched her oval face in the light from the street lamp overhead. "You aren't old enough to have skeletons in your closet."

"I'm twenty-three," she said.

"I'm thirty-nine," he replied. His eyes narrowed. "Sixteen years, little one."

"Fifteen," she murmured breathlessly. "I'll be twenty-four this month."

He caught her eyes and held them for a long time, with the sounds of the night and the city fading into oblivion around them. Her heart swelled, nearly bursting with new, exciting emotions.

"I'll let you do a story," he said finally, "if I get to okay it before it goes into print."

"All right," she replied softly.

"We might as well start early. Are you free in the morning?"

Things were moving so fast she hardly had time to catch her breath, but it was a chance she couldn't pass up. So, ignoring the county commission meeting she was supposed to go to with Bill Peck, she nodded.

"Be in my office at nine a.m. and we'll get started."

"I'll be there." She unlocked her car and got in. "Thanks again for saving me."

"My pleasure," he replied. "Good night."

"Good night." She started the small car and put it in gear. Bryan Moreland was still standing on the sidewalk smoking his cigarette when she rounded the corner.

Three

The excitement was still with her the next morning, when she grabbed her thirty-five millimeter camera and her pad, quickly checking her desk calendar before she started out the door in her usual mad rush. She was neatly dressed in a tweed jacket with a burgundy plaid wool skirt and matching vest, and her small feet were encased in brown suede boots. Bill Peck took in her appearance with a critical eye, and grinned.

"Who are you dressed up for?" he asked pleasantly.

She blushed, hating the color that rushed into her cheeks. "I'm going to interview the mayor," she confessed.

"Oh?" He threw her a questioning glance.

"Well, I do need to do some snooping on the tip I got," she defended, "and I can't help but turn up something if I comb through all the city departments."

"You'll be an old woman by then," he commented. "It's a big city."

"There are only five commissioners over all those departments," she reminded him, "plus a handful of lesser commission posts, like planning and—"

"I know, I know," he said with mock weariness, "don't forget that I had to cover all those groups before you came along to save me.''

''Am I saving you?'' she asked.

He only shook his head, perching himself on the corner of her desk while around him telephones were ringing off the hook. ''I thought the mayor took several bites out of you last night,'' he remarked.

''Only a small one, thanks to you,'' she said dryly.

He shrugged. ''I don't like anyone else taking my lumps.''

''Sure.'' She smiled. ''Anyway, he saved me from a pretty scary gang of toughs last night—two anyway,'' she amended, shivering at the memory. ''For a man his age, he packs a pretty hefty punch.''

His eyes bulged. ''The mayor popped a tough, and you didn't get the story? My God, haven't I taught you anything?''

She glared at him. ''That comes under the heading of my personal business," she told him tightly, "not news."

"But, Carla...he's the mayor, baby, anything he does is news! Think of it like this—Mayor saves reporter in distress!"

"No. Period," she added tightly when he pursued it.

He sighed angrily. "You'll never make a reporter unless you harden up a little."

"If I have to harden up that much, maybe I'll hire on as a hit person for the mob," she said coldly, picking up her camera as she turned to go.

"Wait, Carla," he said quietly and rose to tower over her. "Don't be like that. I was only kidding."

"It didn't sound like it," she replied, casting an accusing glance up at him.

He shrugged, his pale hair catching the light to gleam gold. "I've been at this a long time. I forget sometimes how it is when you're a beginner. Okay, I'll buy that you're trying to get in with His Nibs, and this wouldn't help you break the ice. But," he added darkly, "that's the only reason I'm not doing anything about it. It's news. And news comes before personal privilege. Don't forget it again."

She started to fire back at him, but his face was like stone, and she knew it wouldn't do the slightest bit of good. She turned and walked out without another word.

She stuck her head in the city editor's office, grinning as he looked up from the pile of paper on his desk over the rim of his glasses.

"I'm going to interview the mayor and stop by the financial section to do a little checking, okay?"

"On what we talked about earlier?" Jim Edwards asked with a nod. "Okay. Don't forget that interview with the new city clerk—and get a pix. And see if you can get anything out of Moreland about negotiations on the sanitation strike.''

''I ought to ask Green for that,'' she said with a wry smile.

''When he doesn't even take office until the first?'' he laughed.

''He's officially Public Works Commissioner right now,'' she reminded him, ''regardless of when the next commission meeting is.''

''Touché. He's not a bad man, you know,'' he added quietly. ''Just dedicated.''

''I know. Anything else you want me to check on while I'm there?''

He consulted his sheet. ''Not that I know of. If anything comes up, I'll track you down.''

She knew that already. Edwards had a knack for tracking down his reporters that was nothing short of legendary.

"I'll check back in before I go home," she said.

He nodded, already buried in his copy again.

She only had to wait ten minutes before Bryan Moreland's middle-aged secretary motioned her into his office. He was sitting behind a massive oak desk, his dark eyes stormy, his jaw clenched, when she walked in and sat down, eyeing him cautiously. His big hand was still on the telephone receiver, as if he'd only just finished a telephone call that didn't agree with him.

"Would you rather I come back later?" she asked gently. "Say, in two or three years?"

He took a deep breath, leaned back in the leather-padded executive chair with his hands behind his leonine head, and studied her down his straight nose. "I don't like reporters," he said without preamble.

She grinned. "Neither do I. See, already we've got something in common!"

His hard face relaxed a little. "That was Graham—Dan Graham of the *Sun,* on my neck again for the federal grant for the landfill experiment." He sighed angrily. "If only I could plead justifiable mayhem...."

"Graham thrives on bruises and contusions," she laughed.

"So I hear."

She pulled out her pad and pen, and he watched her curiously.

"I thought modern reporters used tape recorders," he taunted.

"I don't have a lot of luck with machinery," she admitted, peeking up at him. "My car stays in the shop, my hair dryer blows fuses, and I think the garbage disposal ate my cat."

His massive chest shook with deep, soft laughter as he studied her flushed young face with a curious intensity. "What kind of cat was it?" he asked.

"A duke's mixture."

His chiseled mouth curved faintly. "No doubt, if the garbage disposal got him."

"Speaking of garbage," she said quickly, latching onto the subject, "I'd like to know about that new trash-into-power concept."

"It's all still in the planning stages right now," he told her, "but the idea is to take raw garbage and use it to produce power. We're running out of land. And it takes one hell of a lot of land to accommodate the refuse from a population the size of this city's. People don't want to live near sanitary landfills, and they're organized. Obviously, the only answer for the future is recycling."

She scribbled furiously. "And the grant?"

"The planning commissioner knows more about it than I do," he admitted, "but we lined up a matching federal grant and some regional funds to go with it. Give Ed a call; he'll fill you in.''

She raised her eyes from her pad. ''Mr. King isn't my greatest fan,'' she told him. ''I called him last week to ask about the land the planning commission was purchasing for the new airport, and I couldn't even get any figures out of him.''

He shrugged. ''Ed's like me; he doesn't trust newsmen. We've learned to be wary,'' he explained.

She nodded, but her mind was still on King. ''Do you, by any chance, have the figures on the cost of the land?''

His dark eyes narrowed with amusement. ''Don't try to pump me. If you want information on figures, you ask Ed. That's his business at the moment.''

She sighed. ''Fair enough. Anyway, back to the landfill. Doesn't the incinerator tie in to that energy production idea?''

''Honey, you'll need to talk to Tom Green,'' he told her, ''as soon as he's comfortably in office. I'm not that familiar with specific technical aspects of the project. This is one hell of a big city. I'm more concerned with administration and budget than I am with various ongoing projects—outside of my downtown revitalization proposals—and right now I've got all I can do to cope with striking Street Department workers. And the damned horse club wants to hold a parade!''

She smothered a grin. ''You could make the horses wear diapers.''

''Care to apply for the job?'' he asked.

She shook her head. ''I didn't realize how sweeping your responsibilities were. Of course, we do have a strong-mayor system here, but I'm a long way from home, and I tend to forget the size of this city. I suppose that tells you more about my background than a resume.''

''It tells me that you're used to a town of under five thousand, where the mayor can tell you everything that's going on. Right?'' he asked.

''Right. My father owns a weekly newspaper in the southern section of Georgia.''

''Well, this city has almost two million people,'' he elaborated, ''and no city manager. I handle all the administration, greet crown princes, cope with strikes and riots, hire and fire department heads, give the Public Safety commissioner hell twice a day and grant interviews I don't have time for.''

She felt vaguely uncomfortable. ''Sorry. I'll hurry. Can you tell me...''

The intercom buzzed. ''Excuse me,'' Moreland said politely, and leaned to answer it. ''Yes?''

"Bill Harrison on line one," came the reply.

He picked up the receiver. "Hello, Bill, what can I do for you?" he asked pleasantly.

He looked thoughtful, his darkly tanned fingers toying with a fountain pen while he listened to whoever was on the other end—apparently a friend, she surmised. Decision flashed in his dark eyes and he laid the pen down abruptly.

"Tell Carl I'll meet with him and his boys in my office tonight at seven. And try not to leak it to the press, okay?" He cast a speaking glance in Carla's general direction and winked at her lazily. "Thanks, Bill. Talk to you later."

She remembered his invitation to dinner suddenly, and felt a vague prick of disappointment when she realized that the meeting would put an end to that. Although why it should bother her…

"A meeting with the labor leaders?" she probed with a smile.

"Tell your friend Peck he's got a personal invitation. It's going to get a little rough for you, kitten."

"You mean," she said, prickling, "there are actually words I haven't heard?"

His arrogant head lifted. "Woman's libber?" he challenged.

She lifted her own head. "Reporter," she replied. "Sex doesn't have anything to do with it."

A slow, sensuous smile curved his mouth, and his eyes studied her with a bold thoroughness that made her look away in embarrassment. "Doesn't it?" he asked.

She cleared her throat. "Uh, where were we?" she hedged.

The intercom buzzed again. "Phone, Mr. Moreland," his secretary said apologetically. "It's the governor's office calling about that appropriations request you plan to make for inner-city revitalization.''

Moreland picked up the phone. ''Hello, Moreland here,'' he said, leaning forward to study his calendar while he listened and nodded. ''Yes, that's right. Oh, roughly a couple of million. Hell, Ben, you know that's a conservative estimate! Look, I convinced the Nelson companies to invest in cleaning up the fifteen-hundred block on a non-profit basis. They deal in building products. When the slums are cleared out, we'll have to have new housing, right? So the building companies that make this kind of investment ultimately profit from increased sales, do you see the light? All I have to do is convince a few other firms, and I'll have practically all the local funding I need to match an urban redevelopment grant. If you'll do your part, and help me get my paltry two million...''

Carla hid a smile at the disgusted

look on Moreland's dark face. He didn't like opposition—that was evident.

"I know you're having budget problems," Moreland said with magnificent patience. "So am I. But look at it this way, Ben, slums eat up over half my city services. While they're doing that, they pay only around one-twentieth of the real-estate taxes. We have a yearly deficit of twenty-five thousand dollars per acre of slums, Ben. That's a hell of a figure, considering the concentration of them in the downtown area."

He picked up the pen again and twirled it while he nodded. "Yes, I know that. But have you considered how it affects the crime rate here? Slums account for half of all the arrests our policemen make, at least fifty-five percent of all juvenile delinquency. If we can clean up the areas and provide decent housing—give the kids something to do and get them off the streets—God only knows what we could accomplish.''

Whatever he was hearing didn't suit him. The pen snapped in his powerful fingers. "Oh, good God, you mean giving a pencil pusher a two percent increase is worth more than cleaning up my slums? Where the hell is your sense of priorities?''

The answer must have been a good one, because he calmed down. Wearily, he tossed the two halves of the fountain pen onto the desk. "All right, Ben, I'll see what else I can work out before the budget goes into committee. Yes. Thanks anyway.''

He hung up and studied Carla's young face. "Do you like fresh croissants with real butter?''

"Oh, yes!'' she said without thinking.

"Let's go.'' He got up and opened the door for her, waiting while she fumbled to get her camera, purse and accessories together.

"I'm out, if anyone else calls," Moreland told his secretary.

"Yes, Mr. Moreland," she said with a secretive smile.

He led Carla to the elevator and put her in, pushing the first-floor button.

"Where are we going?" she asked breathlessly.

"Away from the telephone," he replied, leaning back against the wall of the elevator to study her. "I feel obligated to answer it as long as I'm sitting at my desk. But I haven't had my breakfast, and I feel like a decent cup of coffee and a roll. Even a mayor has to eat," he added wryly, "although some of my supporters question my right to do that, and sleep, and go home."

"Why don't you eat breakfast?" she asked suddenly.

"Because I don't usually have time

to cook," he replied matter-of-factly. "I have a daily woman who comes in to do the cleaning, but mostly I eat out. I don't like women snooping around my kitchen trying to ingratiate themselves, so I don't keep a full larder."

"Oh," she said noncommittally and let it drop.

He took her to an intimate little coffee house with white linen tablecloths and fresh roses in tiny bud vases and where waltz music danced around them. He sat her down at a small table in the corner and gave the waitress their order.

As she darted away, he pulled a cigarette from his engraved gold case.

"I wish you wouldn't," she said.

He lifted a heavy eyebrow. "I don't gamble, drink to excess, or support organized crime. But I do have this one vice, and you'll notice that the room is quite well ventilated. I don't intend giving up a lifelong habit for the sake of one interview.''

She had the grace to blush. Her eyes moved from the tablecloth to the street outside, where autumn leaves blazed in a tiny maple tree imbedded in concrete, a small colorful reminder of the season. The wind was tumbling fallen leaves and she watched them with a sense of emptiness. She felt as though she'd been alone for a long time.

''What else did you want to ask me?'' he cut into her thoughts.

''Oh!'' She dug her pad and pen out of her purse, moving them aside briefly as the waitress brought china cups filled with freshly brewed imported coffee, fresh croissants and a saucer of creamy butter. ''I wanted to ask about your administration. What was the city's financial situation when you took office, what is it now, what improvements have you made, what goals do you have for the rest of your term in office—that sort of thing.''

He stared at her through a soft cloud of gray smoke. ''Honey, I hope you're not doing anything for the next two weeks, because that's how long it's going to take me to answer those questions.''

She smiled wryly, her pale green eyes catching his. ''Couldn't you manage to do a brief summary in an hour or so?'' she teased.

''Not and do it justice.'' He leaned back in the chair, letting his forgotten cigarette fire curls of gray smoke up toward the ceiling while he took silent inventory of her facial features. ''How old did you say you were?'' he asked.

''Twenty-three,'' she muttered absently, fascinated by his dark, quiet eyes.

''And fresh out of journalism school?'' he probed.

''I got a late start,'' she explained,

crossing her booted legs. "My mother was in poor health. She died." Her eyes went sad at the admission. Two words to describe that long, painful process that ended in death. Words were inadequate.

"A long illness?" he asked, reading her expression as if he could read her mind.

She nodded. "An incurable disease of the central nervous system. There was nothing anyone could do. My father very nearly went under. He had a breakdown, and I had to run the paper until he got back on his feet."

"Quite an experience for you."

"Oh, yes, I learned a lot," she recalled with a dry smile.

"Like what?"

She looked at him sheepishly. "Never misspell a name on the society page."

"What else?"

"Read the copy before you write the

headlines. Don't leave out names in school honor rolls. Never put anything down, because you'll never see it again. And especially never go to a County Commission meeting when they're discussing a new site for the sanitary landfill.''

Both eyebrows went up, and he smiled faintly. ''Lynch mobs?''

''Lynch mobs. I saw in one meeting where sixty people surrounded the sole county commissioner and threatened to shoot him if he put it in their community,'' she recalled. ''I don't suppose you have that kind of problem?''

''No,'' he admitted, ''just dull things like street employee strikes, garbage piling up on sidewalks and into the streets.''

''Why not start a campaign to get everyone in the city to mail their garbage to relatives out of state?'' she suggested.

''Honey, you start it, and I'll personally endorse it," he promised. "Eat your roll before it gets cold."

"Yes, sir," she replied politely.

He glared at her. "I'm not that old."

She peeked at him over the rim of her coffee cup. "Now I know why you brought me here."

He glowered at her. "Why?"

"Real napkins," she explained, "and real cups and saucers. No wasted paper products to fill your garbage trucks!"

He shook his head. "How did you wind up in the city, little country mouse?"

"Dad sold the newspaper and took off on a grand tour of the Orient," she sighed. "I didn't want to go with him, so I caught a plane and came up here to ask one of his former employees for a job."

"And got it, I suppose," he replied, as he took a bite out of his buttered roll.

"Actually, I didn't," she told him

between bites of her own roll. "It was the editor of the Sun, and he didn't have an opening. He sent me to the *Phoenix-Herald*, and I guess they just felt sorry for me. After I told them about my ten starving children and the lecherous landlord…"

"Ten children?" he prompted.

Remembering the tragic death of his daughter, she felt a strangling embarrassment lodge in her throat, and a wild flush stole into her cheeks.

"Don't walk on eggs with me, Carla," he said, using her given name for the first time. "There's nothing to be embarrassed about."

She took a sip of her coffee. "Can you read my mind?" she asked in a small voice.

"Look at me."

She raised her eyes to his and felt them captured, held for ransom by a gaze with the power to stop her heart in mid-beat.

"You have a very expressive face, little one," he said gently. "Readable. Vulnerable."

"I'm as tough as used boots," she murmured.

"Don't bet on it." He finished his coffee. "You realize that damned labor meeting's polished off my dinner invitation?"

"That's all right," she murmured courteously.

"Is it, really?" he asked in a deep, slow voice that sent wild shivers down her straight spine.

She met his searching gaze squarely. "No," she managed shakily, "it isn't."

"Tomorrow?" he asked.

She nodded, and the rush of excitement that made wild lights dance in her eyes was something she hadn't felt since her early teens, her first date.

"I'll call you, in case something comes up." He frowned. "There isn't a boyfriend?"

Her heart went wild; her mouth parted, trembling slightly, drawing his intent gaze before it darted back up to catch the hint of fear in her pale eyes.

"No," she whispered.

Something relaxed in his leonine face, and he smiled at her, an action that made his eyes soft and tender.

"Come on, country mouse. We'll talk on the way back, but I've got a budget meeting at eleven and a luncheon at twelve, followed by a visiting oil magnate at two. In other words," he said as he rose, "I've got to go bridge my credibility gap."

"Thanks for the coffee," she said, moving slowly beside him to the counter.

He glanced down at her. "Your party piece?" he asked softly. "I'm not trying to wheedle any favorable copy out of you, little one. But don't make the mistake of thinking this is just a moment out of time. This is a beginning, Carla.''

The way he said it, and the slow, sweet appraisal his eyes made of her emphasized the underlying comment. She started to speak when she felt his big, warm hand catch hers and press it warmly. And the music danced within her.

Four

She was busily working on the story about the city's new clerk when Bill Peck ambled in and threw himself down in the chair behind his desk.

"God, I'm tired," he groaned. "A delegation of home owners came to the commission meeting to protest a proposed zoning ordinance. It was the hottest meeting I've covered in months."

"Did the ordinance pass?" Carla asked absently as she studied her notes.

"No way. Mass protest does have its advantages," he laughed. "How're you coming on your great expose?"

She hated the mocking note in his voice and gave him a freezing stare. "I don't make fun of your stories," she said accusingly.

He sighed. "Okay, I won't make fun of it. But you're going to have hell pinning anything on the city hall crowd."

"You know!" she burst out.

"I know what you got the tip on, that's all," he replied. "Your mysterious caller got to me last night. But don't make the mistake of taking that kind of tip for gospel. Fired employees tell tales, and I just happened to recognize that one's voice. He's Daniel Brown, a police sergeant who was fired recently for taking payoffs."

"Allegedly taking payoffs," she corrected. "I think he's innocent."

"God, what a babe in the woods you are," he scoffed. "Little girl, don't trust people too far. The city's just full of wolves waiting to pounce on little lambs. I wouldn't put much credibility in Brown's story, either, if I were you."

She didn't mention that she'd already taken her information to the paper's editor and chief counsel and that she had approval from the top to check out that tip. Bill had been a tremendous help to her, boosting her low confidence, building her insight, teaching and encouraging. But he tended to be just the least bit lax in his efforts, and Carla was full of vim and enthusiasm for her job. So she only smiled and agreed with him.

"I hear you had breakfast with the mayor," he said.

"Gosh, news travels fast!" she gasped. "Did you hear that I pushed him under the table and raped him?"

"No, did you?"

She sighed. "Unfortunately the tables are extremely small. But it was a very informative breakfast. For instance,'' she said, leaning on her typewriter to peer at him solemnly, ''did you know that slums account for over fifty percent of city services while they only pay about five to six percent of real-estate taxes?''

He sighed, slumping down in his chair. ''Oh, no, not again,'' he groaned. ''I've heard Moreland's slum removal song until I can sing all twenty choruses!''

''Now, Bill...''

''I don't want to hear it,'' he pleaded.

''But, it's so fascinating,'' she said, and went over to sit on his desk. ''Now just let me lay some statistics on you. For example...'' and she spent the next fifteen minutes describing the downtown revitalization project, only stopping when the city editor stuck his head around the door and reminded her that the deadline was twenty minutes away.

Moreland picked her up at six-thirty for their dinner date, immaculate in his dark evening clothes and a white ruffled shirt that, on him, looked anything except effeminate. He looked sensuous and more than a little dangerous.

Carla smoothed her burgundy velvet dress down over her hips as he closed the door behind him. "I...I hope I'm not underdressed," she murmured.

"You're fine," he said, and his bold eyes added extra approval to the comment.

"I'll get my shawl," she said, turning to retrieve the lacy black creation from her big armchair.

With apparent interest, Moreland was studying a fantasy landscape done by a friend of hers. He turned, eyeing the tastefully decorated apartment with its floral furniture and dark brown carpet. "Earth colors," he murmured.

She smiled. "I like the outdoors."

"So do I. I have a farm out in the metro area," he replied, and she thought how that explained his dark tan. "I'll take you out for the day one weekend."

"Do you have cattle?" she asked him on the way down to the street in the elevator.

"Only a hundred head or so," he replied. "Purebred, mostly, a few crossbreeds. I do it for amusement. My grandfather ranched out west."

"It must take an awfully big horse," she murmured absently, measuring his big, husky frame with her eyes.

A corner of his mouth lifted. "It does. Can you ride?"

"It's been a long time," she admitted, "but I think I could still hold on."

"I've got a gentle little mare you'd like."

"Dogs?" she asked as they walked out onto the sidewalk under the lofty streetlights and neon lights.

"One. A shepherd. The caretaker and his wife look after him for me when I'm here."

"You don't live there?" she asked, amazed.

"I have an apartment a few blocks from my office," he replied. "Some nights I don't finish until midnight. It's an hour's drive to the farm, but that seems like swimming an ocean after a rough day."

She followed him to a low-slung Jaguar XKE and gaped as he unlocked the passenger side. It was black and sleek and looked as if it could race the wind.

He caught the astonishment on her face and smiled faintly.

"What did you expect? A sedate domestic vintage with an automatic transmission? I'm not that old, honey," he said amusedly.

"I wasn't thinking that," she said, dropping down into the plush leather bucket seat. It even smelled expensive. "It isn't conservative."

"Neither am I," he said softly. He closed the door for her and went around the hood to get in behind the wheel. For such a big man, he managed to slide in gracefully.

The statement was easy to believe when she got on the dance floor with him in the very exclusive disco restaurant and went wild trying to keep up with the intricate steps that he managed effortlessly.

"I thought you knew how to do this," he teased when the music stopped momentarily.

She only laughed. "So did I. I'm not in your league!"

"I cheated," he replied. "I took lessons."

She was ashamed to admit that she

had, too. Always graceful on the dance floor, he made her look as if she had two left feet.

But the music was invigorating, and he made dancing fun, so she danced until her legs throbbed with weariness.

Later, he took her to a quiet little bar down the street where they sat sipping drinks over a table where a single candle in a red lamp danced.

"Tired?" he asked.

She nodded with a smile. "Deliciously. It was fun."

He lit a cigarette and smoked quietly. "How did you get into reporting?" he asked.

She watched him leaning back against the booth, and her eyes were drawn involuntarily to his unbuttoned jacket, where the silky shirt was pulled tight across his massive chest. A shadowing of hair was just visible through the thin fabric.

"My father told me not to," she replied in all honesty, keeping her wandering eyes on her glass.

"He didn't want you to follow in his footsteps?"

"He was afraid to let me," she said. Her slender hands fingered the frosty glass. "Dad liked a fight. He wasn't afraid to take on anyone. Crooked politicians, policemen on the take, inept lawmen...anybody. He was threatened a lot, he had tires slashed and windows broken, and once he even got shot at. He's been lucky. He was afraid I might not be."

"Are you afraid?" he asked in a quiet voice.

She didn't dare look up. "A little, sometimes," she admitted. "Controversy is always frightening."

"Why bother with it?"

She smiled. "It's news."

"Do you bleed ink?" he asked conversationally.

"I've never cut myself," she replied saucily.

"Any brothers or sisters?" he probed.

She shook her head and shot him a grin. "They were afraid to try again: they might have had another one like me."

His bold, slow eyes studied her intently from the waist up. "From where I'm sitting, that would have been pretty nice."

She took a long sip of her drink and tried not to blush. He made her feel like a naïve fifteen-year-old.

"What about you?" she asked. "Do you have a family?" Her face blushed as she remembered. "Oh, my…!"

"Don't," he said quietly. "I told you not to walk on eggshells with me. Someone told you about it?"

She nodded miserably.

"The wounds are still there, but not nearly as fresh as they were," he told her. "Sometimes talking about it helps. I loved my daughter very much. I hate to remember how she died, but that doesn't mean I want to forget that she lived. You understand?"

"Yes," she said. "I think I do. Did she look like you? Was she dark?"

A corner of his mouth curved up. "No. She was fair, like her mother. All arms and legs and laughter. Not a sad child at all. She had promise."

Her fingers reached out and touched his, where they rested on the white linen tablecloth. "You miss her."

"Yes," he said simply. He studied her fingers and turned his hand abruptly to catch them in a warm, slow clasp. "Your hands are cool."

"Yours are warm," she replied, feeling the effects of that sensuous clasp all the way to her toes.

His thumb caressed her palm. "We'd better go," he said abruptly, dropping his hand. "It's late, and I've been stuck with a visiting politician first thing in the morning. She wants to see my ghetto.''

''I'd kind of like to see your ghetto, too,'' she remarked.

He smiled at her. ''Be in my office at nine-thirty.''

''Really?''

''What's your city editor going to say? This is the second interview in as many days,'' he said with a wicked smile.

''He'll probably think I'm trying to seduce you,'' she replied smartly.

He studied her in a sudden, tense silence, and she regretted the impulsive teasing as his eyes dropped pointedly to her mouth.

''I don't think you'd know how,'' he said.

She got to her feet, red faced. ''You might be surprised.''

He moved in front of her, forcing her to look up into dark, steady eyes. ''You wear your innocence like a banner,'' he said in a soft, deep voice that reached only her ears.

She tried to answer him, but the words caught in her throat. He seemed to read every thought in her whirling mind.

"I'll get the check," he said, and turned away.

The strained silence was still between them when he pulled up in front of her apartment building and cut the engine.

"Thank you for a lovely evening," she said as she reached for the door handle.

"I'm coming up with you," he said abruptly.

He got out and opened her door for her, eyeing her speechless stare with dawning amusement.

"Don't panic," he teased. "I'm only going to see you safely to your door. I know this city a hell of a lot better than you do, and I just got the revised homicide statistics yesterday.''

She turned and went up the steps with him on her heels. ''Bill Peck was furious at me for not doing a story about the night you rescued me from those punks.''

''Any other reporter would have,'' he reminded her.

She went into the elevator with her green eyes flashing. ''There is such a thing as personal privilege.''

''Not in the eyes of the media,'' he said, joining her. He pressed the sixth-floor button and leaned back. Only the two of them had boarded the conveyance, and she felt very young as he watched her.

''You're nervous,'' he commented.

She ran her tongue over her dry lips. ''Am I?''

One heavy eyebrow went up over dancing dark eyes. ''I almost never rape women in deserted elevators.''

Her face went poinsettia red. "I wasn't..."

"Yes, you were," he mocked. "I'm aware of the dangers even if you aren't, little girl. I didn't plan to pounce on you at your front door."

She studied his face, trying to figure out the enigmatic statement, but it was like reading stone. "Mr. Moreland..."

"My name is Bryan," he corrected, standing aside to let her off the elevator as it stopped on her floor.

"Yes, I know," she murmured, "but it sounds so presumptuous..."

"I won't be ninety for fifty more years," he reminded her.

She laughed in spite of herself. They were at her door now; she turned, looking up at him, and some vague longing nagged in the back of her mind as her eyes swept over his hard, chiseled mouth. She couldn't help wondering if its touch would be rough or tender, and she was suddenly, dangerously, curious....

"Don't forget," he was saying. "Nine-thirty, my office."

"Can I bring a photog?" she asked huskily.

"Bring the whole editorial staff, if you like," he replied amiably. "It's my favorite story, and I love to tell it."

"Thanks again for tonight."

"My pleasure, country mouse," he said with a quiet smile. "Good night."

"Good night," she replied nervously.

His dark eyes dropped to her mouth, then slanted up to catch the mingled curiosity and apprehension in her shy gaze. He smiled mockingly just before he turned and walked away.

She lay awake half the night wondering why he hadn't kissed her. It would have been the normal end to an evening. It was customary. But he'd only smiled, and left her, not even both-

ering to brush a kiss against her forehead.

Was something wrong with her?
Wasn't she pretty enough, attractive
enough to appeal to him? Or did he already have a girlfriend? The question
tortured her. He had women, she realized. He was certainly no monk. But
why had he asked her out in the first
place, and what did he really think of
her? Had it all been a ploy to get her
interested in his urban renewal program?

Bryan Moreland was one puzzle she
couldn't seem to put together, and he
got more complicated by the day.

Bill Peck gave her an odd look the
next morning when she explained why
she couldn't attend a City Planning
Commission session with him.

''We've done three pieces on that
damned downtown revitalization theme
of his already,'' he said dourly. ''Don't

you think he's had enough free publicity?"

"I'm working on a story, in case you've forgotten," she replied, irritated.

"A story? Or the mayor?" he returned.

She gathered her purse and camera and went toward Edwards' office in a smouldering fury.

"I'm gone," she told him.

"Wait a sec. Come in and close the door," he called.

She shut out the sounds of typewriters and ringing telephones. "What's up?"

He motioned her to a chair. "Suppose you tell me that," he replied.

Her brows came together. "I don't understand."

"Moreland took you out. Then, this bogus story this morning— Carla, you're not getting involved with him, are you?" he asked kindly.

"Why...no," she lied. "But, he isn't even involved..."

"Your informant called me this morning."

"Is he after a job?" she asked with a flare of anger. "First Bill, now you...is he going to call everyone on the staff?"

"He knows you're seeing Moreland," he replied calmly, leaning back in his chair, "and he thinks the mayor may be involved in this."

She felt something inside her freeze. A cold, merciless, nameless something that had been in bud.

"He isn't," she said.

"How could you possibly know? Be reasonable. You haven't even been able to get to the records."

She clutched her purse in her lap, her eyes staring at the skirt of her simple beige dress as she fought for control.

"All we know for sure," she replied, "is that land was purchased by the city for a new airport. The evaluation was twenty-five thousand dollars an acre—a steal even though it was in a sparsely populated section. But the city paid a half million for it.'' She sighed. ''It's not unusual for a realtor to mark up his asking price when he knows he has a buyer like the city. But Daniel Brown said that the land owner only received two-hundred-fifty-thousand dollars and that records will bear him out. The problem,'' she added ruefully, ''is that when I asked for the records of the transaction, that icy-voiced little financial wizard promptly called the city attorney and they refused to let me see the records on the grounds that it hadn't been formally approved by the city council.''

''That's a lie,'' Edwards said.

She nodded. ''I know, and I told the city attorney so. But we did a piece on his department last month that he didn't like, and he can quote the obscure law to you verbatim if you call and ask him.''

"God deliver me from disgruntled lawyers!'' he groaned.

"It doesn't matter,'' she said. ''I'm going to ask the mayor for permission to look at them.'' She smiled. ''I think he'll agree.''

He eyed her. "Unscrupulous little minx.''

''Me?'' she blushed.

''You. Get out of here. And if you don't have any luck with Moreland, I'll get our legal staff on it.''

''No problem.''

She walked out the door in a daze. Was she trying to get close to Moreland to get information? It might have been that way at the beginning. But not anymore. She remembered what Edwards had said about Moreland being involved in what could be the biggest city scandal since the City Council chairman was arrested picking up a streetwalker. It couldn't be true. Not Bryan Moreland. Perhaps Edwards had misunderstood Brown. She smiled. She'd have a talk with the ex-cop tomorrow. It was about time she got the whole story firsthand.

Moreland was waiting for her in his office with a woman she recognized as the new mayor of a city in a neighboring state: Grace Thomas.

"Grace, this is Carla Maxwell," he told the older woman, "with the *Phoenix-Herald*. She's going to do a follow-up on the revitalization."

"Nice to meet you," Grace said with a pleasant smile. She was years older than Carla, a contemporary of Moreland's most likely, despite her dark brown hair that didn't show a trace of gray. "I'm very interested in the renewal idea. It might be feasible in my own city."

"If you're both ready, let's get moving," Moreland said as he helped Grace on with her plush wool coat. "I've got a budget meeting in two hours, and that doesn't leave us much time."

Carla watched the way the older woman's eyes slid sideways to Moreland as he held her coat, and she wanted to drop her heavy camera on the woman's foot. It was ridiculous to feel this surge of jealousy toward the visiting mayor. After all, she wasn't even pretty, and she was wearing a wedding ring! But that didn't stop her from wanting to push Moreland away from her.

Inexplicably, Moreland looked up at that moment and caught the expression on her face, and something darkened his eyes.

She averted her gaze quickly while Mrs. Thomas went right on talking about her city council woes without even noticing the undercurrents around her.

Walking through the streets with

Moreland and City Planning Commission Chairman Ed King and the two other commission members, Carla was impressed with plans to renovate the run-down area. While Mrs. Thomas pumped King, Moreland dropped back beside Carla.

"Interesting, isn't it?" he asked quietly, indicating the windowless old houses with their sagging porches and littered yards. Some were deserted, but children played aimlessly in the yards around others, and deserted store buildings were interspersed with the homes.

"Tragic," she replied. "It reminds me of shacks I've seen back home. Poverty has many addresses."

"Yes," he replied.

"Is this area where you're concentrating?" she asked as she paused to photograph a house with blackened, paneless windows where a little girl stood, ragged and barefoot, clinging to a post.

"Yes. I got a manufacturing chain to bear almost half the cost of construction; their headquarters office is located near here. When we get this project going, you won't recognize the neighborhood."

"How about the people?" she asked, gazing up at him. "You can change their environment, but can you change them? Poverty doesn't go away because the setting is changed. How about employment?"

He smiled. "One step at a time, honey. I've got experts working on that aspect of it."

She glanced ahead, where Mrs. Thomas had cornered Ed King and his two planners. "Why won't your legal department let me look at the airport land purchase records?" she asked suddenly, catching his eyes.

Both heavy brows went up, and he paused before he replied, "Honey, that's between you and Ed King. I've

told you before, I'm not going to inter-
fere."

"But..."

He turned away. "We'd better catch
up."

She followed along, puzzled and a
little disappointed at the answer he'd
given her. And try as she might, a nagging suspicion began to work on her
mind.

"Mr. King tells me that the slums
account for half of all your arrests,"
Mrs. Thomas was saying as they
walked.

"That's right," Moreland agreed.
"And fifty percent of all disease, as
well as thirty-five percent of all fires.
With proper housing, we could save almost a million dollars a year in fire
losses and communicable disease."

Carla found herself beside Ed King,
and the mayor's voice faded in her ears
as she put the question to the planning

commissioner. "May I ask you a question, Mr. King?" she asked abruptly.

He glanced at her, eyes sharp through his heavy glasses. His bald head gleamed in the cold sunlight. "If it concerns the airport land purchase, I'm sure the city attorney told you that the information is privileged until the council formally approves the purchase."

"Excuse me," she countered coolly, "but the council approved the purchase two meetings ago," she snapped her notebook closed, "and construction on the terminal is already underway."

"You choose to misunderstand me," he said with a cold smile. "the council hasn't approved the paperwork. A formality, of course, but legally binding. Check the city charter."

"I have," she told him, her green eyes narrowed. "If everything is up and aboveboard, Mr. Chairman, why all the secrecy?"

He purpled. "As usual, you reporters want to make something of nothing! I've told you, it's a formality, the figures will be released."

"When?" she shot back.

"Carla!" Moreland stopped speaking in the middle of a sentence to thunder her name. She jumped, turning to face him. "That's enough, by God," he growled. "This isn't an interrogation."

The clipped, measured tones made her flinch. "I apologize," she said tightly. "I didn't mean…"

"If you'll excuse me, Bryan," King said curtly, "I think I'll pass on the rest of the tour. You know my position."

"Sure," Moreland said. "We'll talk later."

"A pleasure to meet you, Mrs. Thomas," King told the visiting mayor with a smile. He ignored Carla as he walked away, taking his planners with him.

"Well," Mrs. Thomas said with a

mirthless laugh, "I suppose that little scene ended my chances of a discussion with your planners."

Carla flushed to the roots of her hair. She pressed her camera close to her side. "I...I have an interview with the public works commissioner at eleven," she said unsteadily. "I'd better get going. Thanks for the tour."

She almost ran for her car, deaf to Moreland's deep voice calling her name.

She was shaking all over by the time she got to Tom Green's office. He was a public accountant, and she had a feeling he'd made a good commissioner, if for no better reason than his outspokenness.

At least, she thought wearily as she waited in his outer office, he wouldn't be angry. She could still see Bryan Moreland's dark, accusing eyes. Why, oh, why did she have to open her big mouth? It was all part of the job, but the argument had left a bad taste in her mouth, along with Moreland's obvious disapproval.

"Miss Maxwell?" the secretary repeated. "You can go in now."

She put on her best smiling face and went into Tom Green's carpeted office.

He rose, tall and gray haired, towering over her as he shook her hand. "I have to agree that the media gets prettier every day," he said with an approving glance from pale blue eyes.

She smiled. "For that, I promise to mail all my garbage out of town."

"God bless you. How about agreeing to support my recycling concept instead?" he teased. "I can get federal funding and match services instead of cash."

"Really?" she asked, sidetracked. She whipped out her pad and pen. "Tell me about it."

He did, and by the time he was

through, her cold hands had warmed and she was relaxed.

"You were tense when you came in," he observed. "Care to tell me why? Surely it wasn't because I inspire fear in young women?"

"I...uh, I just had a run-in with the planning commissioner," she said. "Nothing important."

"Ummm," he said noncommittally. "I never approved of Moreland making that appointment," he said bluntly. "King was a real-estate agent before he took office, you know. A damned shady one, if you want my opinion. He gave it up when he went into office, but I'll bet my secretary that he still has all his old contacts. It just isn't good business. He has too much sway with the city commission, what with Moreland on such friendly terms with him."

"Are they friends?" she asked carelessly.

"They were in the service together,"

he replied. "I thought you knew all that."

"I'm new in town," she said, and let it go at that.

She walked back to her office in a silence fraught with concern. So many things were beginning to make sense: for instance, King's real-estate background. Was he somehow involved in that missing money? Was Bryan Moreland involved? Her eyes closed momentarily. Bryan! He'd probably never speak to her again after the confrontation she'd had with his friend. Perhaps it was for the best. She was getting involved with him—too involved. And she didn't dare.

She handed in her copy and went home, turning down Bill Peck's offer of a free meal. She didn't feel like company, and she didn't want to be pumped about her latest information. That was all Bill was after, she knew. She couldn't have borne talking about it.

The apartment seemed lonelier than ever as she dressed idly in a pair of worn jeans and a blue ribbed top that was slightly too small. She turned on the radio and as pleasant, soft music filled the apartment, she went into the small kitchen to whip up an omelet. She was going to have to force it down, at that. Food was the last thing on her mind.

The doorbell was an unwelcome interruption. The omelet was almost done, and she had to turn it off before time was up. Grumbling, she moved irritably to the door. It was probably some student selling magazine subscriptions. The apartment house was a prime target, despite the "no soliciting" signs, and she was in no mood for a sales pitch.

She swung open the door with unnecessary force and froze with her mouth open to speak. Bryan Moreland was standing there, idly leaning against the wall, his dark eyes pointedly studying the too-tight top she was wearing.

Five

He smiled at the expression on her face. "Who were you expecting?" he asked.

She swallowed. "Not you," she said without thinking. He was wearing slacks and an open-necked burgundy velour shirt that bared a sensuous amount of hair-roughened bronzed flesh.

"Why?"

"Well…"

"You might as well invite me in," he told her. "I've got a feeling it won't be a short explanation."

"Oh!" She opened the door wider and stepped aside to let him in beside her. He went straight to the armchair by the window and lowered his big body into it.

"Would you like some coffee?" she asked, stunned by his sudden appearance.

"If you can spare it," he replied with a wry smile. "I just put the lady mayor on a plane. I haven't even had lunch yet. That's why I came. I thought you might like to go out for a burger and fries."

It was almost laughable, the mayor taking a reporter out for a hamburger.

"Well, I…" she stammered.

"Aren't you hungry?" he asked. "Or are you still smarting from that round with Ed?"

She lowered her eyes. "I didn't mean to ruin your tour."

He laughed. "My God, is that why you ran away?"

"I thought you were angry with me," she admitted.

"I was furious. But that was this morning, and this is now," he explained quietly. "I don't hold grudges. You and Ed can damned well fight it out, but not on my time. Now do you want supper or not?"

She looked up, studying him. "I just cooked an omelet."

"Big enough for two?" he teased.

She nodded. "I can make some toast."

"How about cinnamon toast?" he asked, rising. "I'm pretty good at it."

"You can cook?" she asked, forgetting that she looked like something out of a ragbag, that she wasn't wearing makeup and her long hair was gathered back with a rubber band in a travesty of a ponytail.

"My mother thought it would be a good idea if I learned," he recalled with an amused smile. "She gives me a refresher course every year at Christmas."

"What else can you cook?" she asked, leading the way into the small kitchen.

"The best pepper steak you've ever tasted."

"I don't believe you."

"Come to dinner Sunday," he said, "I'll prove it."

"At your apartment?" she asked as she handed him the bread and a cookie sheet spread with aluminum foil.

"At the farm. I'll pick you up early in the morning, and you can spend the day."

She thought for a minute, feeling herself sinking into deep water. She'd been too pleased at the sight of him tonight, too happy that he'd bothered to come and ask her out.

He came up behind her; and with a quick-silver thrill of excitement, she felt his big, warm hands pressing into her tiny waist. "I have a housekeeper, Mrs. Brodie. She's elderly and buxom, and she'll cut off my hands if I try to seduce you. Satisfied, Miss Purity?"

She felt her color coming and going as he drew her closer, his breath whispering warmly in her hair.

"I...I wasn't worried about that," she managed weakly.

Deep, soft laughter rumbled in the chest at her back. "Do you think I'm too old to feel desire?" he asked.

"Mr. Moreland!" she burst out.

"Make it Bryan," he said.

"Bryan," she repeated breathlessly.

"Why aren't there any men in your life?" he asked suddenly. "Why don't you date?"

Her eyes closed against the memory. "I date you," she corrected weakly.

"Before me there was someone. Who? When?" he asked harshly, his fingers biting into her soft flesh. "Tell me!"

"He was married," she said miserably.

There was a long, heavy silence behind her. "Did you know?"

She shook her head. "I was just nineteen, and horribly naïve. I met him while I was a freshman in college. He was one of the instructors. We went together for two months before I found out."

She felt him tense. "How far had it gone?"

She shifted restlessly. "Almost too far," she admitted, remembering the phone call that had saved her virtue. A phone call from his wife, and she'd answered the phone...

"And you gave up on life because of one bad experience?" he asked quietly.

"I learned not to trust men," she corrected, bending her head. "It was... safer...to stay at home, unless I was with girl friends."

"And now, Carla?" he persisted.

She chewed on her lower lip nervously. "I...don't know."

His hand slid down her hips, pulling her back closer to him. Involuntarily, her hands went to push against the intimacy of his, and he laughed.

"Turn on the broiler for me," he said, releasing her. "That omelet's going to be stone cold."

She obeyed him mindlessly, fighting down her confusion.

They ate in a companionable silence, and she felt his dark eyes watching her when she wasn't watching him. Something was happening between them. She could feel it, and it frightened her.

Afterward, she put the dishes in the

sink to soak, refusing his offer of help to wash them, and led the way into the living room nervously.

"I can't stay," he said. "I've got to stop in at a cocktail party later tonight to try and twist the governor's arm for emergency funding for my revitalization."

"Dressed like that?" she asked without thinking.

"It's informal," he teased. His dark, bold eyes traveled down the length of her slender body. "You look pretty informal yourself."

"I wasn't expecting company."

"Sorry I came?" he asked bluntly.

"No," she replied.

His jaw tightened, and she saw a strange darkness grow in his eyes as he looked at her. He held her gaze until she thought her heart was going to burst, until the only sound she could hear was the wild beating of her own heart.

"Good night, Carla," he said abruptly and, turning, went out the door without a backward glance.

She stood exactly where she was and caught her breath. He hadn't wanted to go out that door. She'd read it in his eyes. But he hadn't kissed her. He still hadn't kissed her.

"What's wrong with me?" she asked the room unsteadily, turning to look in the mirror. But all she saw was a disappointed face and a body in a too-tight blouse. The reflection told her nothing.

She had Daniel Brown, the informant, meet her for coffee the next afternoon in the small international coffee house where she had gone with Moreland that first time. Brown was a personable young man with an honest face, but she didn't quite like the way his blue eyes darted away while he spoke.

"Did you know that the mayor and

James White were close friends?" he asked as they sat and drank coffee at a corner table.

She stared at him. "James White? Isn't he that rich realtor who was investigated for fraud last year?"

"The same. Do a little digging, and you may come up with some interesting little tidbits."

"Why are you furnishing all this information so generously?" she asked abruptly.

He looked uncomfortable. "I don't like corruption," he replied.

"Is that the truth?" she probed, "or are you just trying to get back at the people who helped you out of your job?"

He shrugged. "It's a dog-eat-dog world."

"Sometimes," she agreed. "Why do you think Moreland's involved?"

"He's got too much money showing to be a mayor," he replied vaguely.

"So he has. But I understood he was independently wealthy."

"Did you?" he asked. "You're seeing a lot of him lately."

"I'm working on a story," she said for the second time, to the second person, that week.

"He wasn't much of a husband," he said with a strange bitterness. "Don't get your hopes up in that direction, either."

She stood up. "My personal life is my own business."

"That's what you think." He sipped his coffee. "Check out White. You'll see."

She turned on her heel and left him there. Late that afternoon, she took her wealth of bits and pieces to Edwards and requested that he give it to the paper's attorneys and see if they could force the city attorney to release the airport land purchase records.

* * *

Bryan Moreland's farm was like a picture postcard. Well-kept grounds, white-fenced paddocks, silver silos, a red barn with white trim, and a farmhouse with a sprawling front porch and urns that must have been full of flowers in the spring and summer.

Mrs. Brodie grinned from ear to ear when Moreland brought Carla in and introduced her. The buxom old woman obviously approved, and the table she set for lunch was evidence of it. Carla ate until her stomach hurt, and Mrs. Brodie was still trying to press helpings of apple cobbler on her.

Moreland helped her escape into his study, where a fire was blazing in the hearth. It was a dreary day outside, drizzling rain and cold. But the den, with its oriental rug and sedate dark furniture, was cozy. She stared at the portrait above the white mantel curiously. It was a period painting, and the man in it looked vaguely like Bryan Moreland.

"Is he a relative?" she asked.

He tossed two big, soft cushions down on the floor in front of the hearth and stretched out with his hands under his head. "In a manner of speaking," he replied lazily. "He was my grandmother's lover."

She blushed, and he laughed.

"And the picture hangs in here?" she asked, aghast.

"He's something of a family legend," he replied. "He'd be damned uncomfortable in the closet. Come here," he added with a sensuous look in his dark eyes as he gestured toward the pillow next to his.

She hesitated, drawn by the magnetism of his big body in the well-fitted brown trousers and pale yellow velour shirt, but wary of what he might expect of her.

His dark eyes took in the length of

her body, lingering on the plunging V-neck of her white sweater, tracing her dark slacks down to her booted feet.

"If we make love," he said quietly, "I won't let it go too far. Is that what you're afraid of, Carla?"

She caught her breath. He seemed to read her mind. She only nodded, lost for words.

His eyes searched hers. "Then, come on."

She eased down beside him, curling her arms around her drawn-up knees with the pillow at her back. "Are we?" she asked huskily.

He traced the line of her spine with deft, confident fingers. "Are we what?" he asked deeply.

"Going to make love," she managed shakily.

"That depends on you, country mouse," he said matter-of-factly, and he removed his caressing hand.

She half-turned and looked down at

him. His eyes were dark, smouldering, and there was no smile to ease the intensity of his piercing gaze.

"If you want it, come here," he said gruffly.

She didn't even think. She went down into his outstretched arms as if she were going home, as if she'd waited all her life for a big, husky, dark man to hold out his arms to her.

He crushed her against his broad chest and lay just holding her as the fire crackled and popped cheerfully in the dimly lit room.

"It's been a long time for me, Carla," he said in a strange, gruff tone. "Kisses may not be enough."

She felt her body stiffen against him. "I can't..."

"Don't start freezing on me," he said at her ear. "I'm not going to throw you over my shoulder and beat a path to my bedroom with you."

"But you said..." she whispered.

"I may touch you," he murmured sensuously. His mouth brushed lazily, warmly, at her throat, while his big hands worked some magic on her back through the sweater. "Like this." He eased his hands underneath it, against the silken young flesh of her bare back. "And this," he added, sweeping his hands up to her shoulder blades, discovering for himself that she was wearing nothing under the sweater.

"No..." she whispered unsteadily, a protest that sounded more like a moan.

His thumbs edged out under her arms, brushing against flesh that had never known a man's hands, and she caught her breath at the sensations it fostered.

"I want to love you," he said softly. He eased her back on the rug, with her head and shoulders against the pillow, letting his hands move very gently on her rib cage in a silence burning with emotions.

"Bryan..." she whispered achingly.

He bent, and his mouth parted slightly as it touched hers in soft, slow movements. It was torture, the teasing, brushing touch of his mouth and hands, a delicious torment that made her heart beat violently against the walls of her chest. She had never wanted anything as desperately as she now wanted Bryan, and in a fever of wanting, she heard her own voice shatter as she cried out for his touch.

His mouth took hers violently, hungrily, pressing her head deep into the pillow while his hands taught her sensations so exquisite, she arched submissively toward them.

Once her eyes slid open to look up into his, and he smiled at the awe and emotion in them—a smile that was strangely tender and soft with triumph.

He drew her own hands to the buttons of his shirt and watched while she undid them, clumsily, because she was shaking from the lazy caresses of his deft hands.

"Here," he said quietly, drawing her mouth to his chest. "Like this. Hard, honey, hard!" he whispered huskily as her mouth brushed against the warm flesh that smelled of spice and soap.

She reached up to draw his mouth back down to hers and felt a shudder run through him as his body moved over hers in a way that was pleasure beyond bearing.

He hurt her mouth, bruised it, as all his hard control seemed to disappear at her yielding. He drew back suddenly, and his dark eyes were smouldering with hunger as they looked down into hers.

"I want you like hell," he said in a rough whisper. "Another minute of this and I'm going to take you. Is that what you want, Carla?"

Sanity came back in a blazing rush. She gasped at the emotions that lay raw and bruised at the harshness of his statement.

"No," she said shakily. "No, it isn't. Bryan, I'm sorry…"

He rolled away from her and got to his feet. He went straight to the bar and poured himself a large whiskey, downing it before he lit a cigarette—all without looking at her.

She pulled down her sweater and got to her feet, her tongue gingerly touching her bruised mouth. She felt vaguely ashamed at her abandon, and as she stared at his broad back, she couldn't help wondering if he thought she was like this with other men. In fact, she'd never let any man touch her like that. She was at a loss to explain why it had seemed so right when Bryan had done it. Her face flamed at the memory.

"I'll take you home," he said coldly. "Get your coat."

"Bryan…" she began apologetically.

He turned, and his eyes were blazing. "Get your damned coat," he said, in a voice that froze her.

Fighting tears, she gathered her possessions and followed him out to the car.

Six

She went around in a brown mood for the next week, alternately crying and cursing her own stupidity for getting herself emotionally involved with a man who only wanted one thing of her.

In between the tears, she waited vainly for the phone to ring, jumping every time it trilled, only to find some routine caller on the other end. The doorbell only rang once in all that time, and she dashed for it, her heart racing, only to find a neighbor inviting her to a rent party for another neighbor down on his luck.

How, she wondered, could she have thought Moreland was as involved as she was? Just because he took her out a few times didn't mean he wanted to marry her. She knew that, but had she really mistaken his objectives that much? All along, had he only been angling for a way to get her into his bed?

She could still blush, remembering the way it had been between them, that strange look in his eyes as they met hers while her body seemed to belong to someone else in her wild abandon. She wasn't easy, she wasn't! But, apparently, he thought so; and she still felt the whip of his anger even now, his smouldering silence as he'd driven her home and left her there, without even a word of apology. She hadn't been crying, but surely he could have seen that she was about to. Or perhaps he had. Perhaps it just hadn't mattered to him one way or the other.

That was the hardest thing to face; the fact that he just didn't care at all, except in a purely physical sense.

"No date with the mayor today?" Bill Peck chided as she sat down at her desk on Friday morning with an increasingly familiar listlessness.

She wanted to pick up something and throw it at him, but she kept cool. "I was writing a story," she reminded him. "It's finished."

"And it's been lying on Edwards' desk for the past week, where it will probably be lying this time next year," he reminded her. "The revitalization story's been done to death, and you know it. What's the matter, honey, did your big romance go sour?"

She whirled, her green eyes flashing as they met his calculating ones. "You go to hell," she flashed in a tight, controlled voice. "What I do and how I do it are no concern of yours. I don't work for you; I work with you, and don't you ever forget it!"

A slow, mischievous smile appeared on his face, causing her anger to eclipse into puzzlement.

"That's my girl," he chuckled.

She slammed a pencil down on her spotless desk. "You beast!" she grumbled.

"It's my middle name. Now, are you finally back to normal? Business as usual?" He grabbed his coat. "Come on, we've got a press conference this morning. I've already cleared it with Eddy."

Eddy was his nickname for the city editor, and if Eddy said okay, she had no choice. But she got her purse and camera together with a sense of foreboding. "A press conference where?" she asked carefully.

"At city hall, where else?"

She froze, desperately searching her mind for an excuse, any excuse to get out of it. Another meeting. There had to be another meeting or an interview or a picture—oh, God, there had to be something!

"I said, let's go," Peck said, taking her arm. "You haven't got an excuse. I need some pix, and I can't handle a camera with this finger," he added, holding up a bandaged right forefinger. "I cut it on a sheet of bond paper, can you imagine?" he sighed. "Worse than a knife cut."

"Can't you take Freddy?" she asked hopefully.

"What's the matter?" he asked with a sideways glance. "Afraid of him?"

She knew exactly what he meant, and she wanted to admit that she was terrified. She almost put it into words, but just at the last minute, she stopped herself.

"I'm not afraid of anybody," she

said instead. "My father said it was better to go through life giving ulcers than letting other people give them to you."

"Wise man," he grinned. "On a trip to the Orient, did you say?"

It was just the question she needed to start her talking, and to take her mind off Moreland. They were in the elevator at city hall before she realized what Peck had been doing.

"You did that on purpose," she accused gently.

He glanced down at her, cocking his hat at an angle over his pale brow. "Who, me?"

"Yes, you, you lovely man."

He grinned at her. "Like to adopt me?"

"No. You're too tall."

He squatted down a little. "How about now?"

"Lose a hundred pounds, and we'll talk about it," she assured him.

The conference room was crowded, but she didn't spend one second looking around for Bryan Moreland. She took a seat beside Peck in the back section and lowered her eyes to her camera, keeping them down resolutely while she pretended to fiddle with light settings.

"You don't think you're going to get me a shot from here, do you?" Peck asked as he sat down beside her.

"I'll use the telescopic lens," she said under her breath. All around them, news people were milling around. A couple of them, radio reporters whom she recognized from other stories, called to her, and she managed a frozen smile and a tiny wave of her hand in response.

"What in hell is the matter with you?" Peck asked. "You look like you're trying to get smaller."

"Will you please shut up?" she begged. His voice was loud, and it carried. "Please sit down and pretend we aren't acquainted."

"But we work for the same paper," he argued.

"Not for long, if you keep this up," she whispered back.

"You *are* scared of him!"

"Shut up," she said through her teeth, making a prayer of it as Bryan Moreland's big, husky form came into view. He swept the room with his dark, cutting gaze, and she felt the impact of it like a physical blow when his eyes stopped on her averted face. She stared straight ahead, ignoring him, while her heart felt as if it were going to jump out of her body.

She didn't look at him again until he was at the podium, with the City Council and the City Planning Commission gathered around the conference table with him. She recognized Edward King and Tom Green immediately.

"What's this all about?" she asked Peck in a muted whisper.

"The airport," he replied with a grin. "You made somebody take notice with that run-in with King, didn't you?"

She shifted restlessly and forced herself to listen to Moreland's deep curt voice describing plans for the new airport and the expansion of services it would mean by national airlines. For the first time, the city would have an international airport; a tribute to its rapid growth.

But when he finished, the land purchase still hadn't been discussed, and she noticed that the mayor didn't throw the floor open for questions, as he usually did at the end of a press conference.

She got her things together and started to dart out the side door, but Bill Peck left her, calling back that he had to talk to Tom Green, and Carla got trapped between the nest of chairs and a group of news people passing tidbits of information back and forth. The next thing she knew, she was looking up into Bryan Moreland's dark, quiet eyes.

Her heart dropped, and she could feel her knees trembling. She let her gaze fall to his burgundy tie.

"Good morning, your honor," she said with a pitiful attempt at lightness.

"Five days, two hours, twenty-six minutes," he said quietly.

She looked up, feeling all the dark clouds vanish, all the color come back into her colorless world as she realized the meaning behind the statement.

"And forty-five seconds," she whispered unsteadily.

He drew in a hard, deep breath, and she noticed for the first time how haggard he looked, how tired. "Oh, God, I've missed you," he said in a voice just loud enough to carry to her ears and no further. "I wanted a hundred times to call you and explain…I know what you must have thought, and you couldn't have been further off base. But I got busy… Oh, hell have supper with me. I'll try to put it into words.''

The need to say yes was incredible. But she was cautious now, wary of him. He could hurt her now, because he could get close, and she wasn't sure she was willing to take the risk a second time.

He read that hesitation and nodded. ''I know what you're afraid of. But trust me this once. Just listen to me.''

She shifted and let a long breath seep out between her lips. ''All right.''

''I'll pick you up at six.''

She nodded her assent and looked up, hypnotized by the strange expression in his eyes.

''Don't look at me like that,'' he whispered deeply. ''There are too many cameras in here.''

She knew what he meant without any explanation, and her face colored again.

''Reading my mind?'' he asked with a wicked smile as his eyes dropped to the soft, high curve of her breasts. ''Read it now.''

She pulled her coat tight around her and tried to breathe normally. ''I...I'll see you later, then,'' she managed weakly.

He chuckled softly as he moved to let her pass by him. His eyes didn't leave her until she was out of sight.

She was like a teenaged girl on her first date, waiting for him that night with her hair hanging loose over her shoulders, the single green velour evening gown she owned, clinging to her slender curves like a second skin, bringing out the soft tan of her bare arms and shoulders.

She couldn't help feeling nervous. What was he going to expect from her now? The fact that he'd missed her hadn't really changed anything. And what about her? What was she willing to give? What did she truly feel?

In the midst of her mental interrogation, the doorbell screamed into the silence, and she jumped just before she ran to answer it.

He walked in by her even as she opened the door, his scowl fierce, his eyes dangerous.

"Hard day?" she asked softly.

"They're all hard," he said, turning to look down at her. The anger drained out of his hard face as he studied her soft curves with an expression that grew warmer, possessive, as the seconds throbbed past.

His massive chest rose and fell heavily under his dark evening clothes, his ruffled silk shirt. "Oh, honey," he said finally, deeply, "that is one hell of a dress."

"Do you really like it?" she murmured inanely, speaking for the sake of words, while her eyes told him something very different.

"I hope you haven't gone to any great pains with your makeup, little girl," he said finally, moving closer, "because I'm about to smear the hell out of it."

Her lips parted under a rush of breath while he pulled her against his big body, molding her slowly against him.

"It's been too long already," he said in a harsh whisper, bending his dark head until she felt the warm, uneven pulse of his breath against her trembling lips. "I can't get that evening out of my mind, Carla...."

His mouth hurt. It was as if the hunger he felt made violence necessary, and his big arms bruised in their ardor while he took what he needed from her soft ardent mouth.

"Sleep with me," he whispered against her mouth. "I need you."

"Bryan..." she breathed, drawing back as far as the crush of his arms would allow.

"God, don't make me wait any longer," he growled unsteadily. "I'm so hungry for you I can hardly stay alive for wanting you. Carla, little Carla, why are you holding back? You won't regret it."

She swallowed and her eyes closed. "Bryan, there's never been a man," she said in a haunted voice.

She felt his arms stiffen around her, felt his breath catch.

"What did you say?" he asked.

She drew a steadying breath. "I said, I've never slept with a man."

"But, at the farm... My God, woman, you were on fire..."

Her eyelids pressed hard together as a wave of embarrassment swept over her, and her pale cheeks colored. "I know. But it's still true."

There was a long pause, and then his

big, warm hands came up to force her face out of hiding, so that he could search it and her misty eyes.

"It was the first time for you... touching, being touched?" he asked finally, and there was a new tenderness in his voice.

All she could manage to do was nod. Her throat felt as if it had been glued shut.

The hard lines in his face relaxed, smoothed out. He looked at her as if he'd never seen a woman before. His dark eyes went down to her soft body, lingering on the high young curves that his fingers had touched so intimately.

"I remember looking down at you," he said absently, "and there was an expression on your face I couldn't understand. Now it all makes sense."

She chewed on her lower lip, vaguely embarrassed, because she remembered that moment, too—vividly.

He turned away, ramming his big

hands into his pockets with a heavy sigh. "Well, that tears it," he said roughly.

She stared at his broad back, her eyes drawn to the thick, silver-threaded hair that gleamed like black diamonds in the overhead light.

"I'm sorry," she murmured inadequately.

"My God, for what?" he asked harshly, whirling to face her. His dark eyes blazed across the room.

The question stunned her. In the sudden silence, she could hear the ticking of the clock by the sofa, the sounds of traffic in the street as if they were magnified.

"Are you trying to apologize to me for not being the woman I thought in my arrogance that you were?" he asked, a new gentleness in his voice. "I don't want that."

She swallowed, dreading the question even as she asked it. "What *do* you want?"

A wisp of a smile turned up one corner of his sensuous mouth. "I could answer that in a monosyllable," he teased, watching the color come and go in her cheeks. "But, I won't." He shot back his white cuff and glanced at his watch. "We'd better get moving, honey. I ordered the table for seven-thirty, sharp. Ready?"

Confused by his sudden change of mood, she nodded absently and went to get her long black coat with its lush mink collar—an extravagance she'd once regretted.

He opened the door for her but caught her gently by the arm as she started out.

"I'm glad the first time was with me," he said in a strange, low tone.

Her face went beet red. She couldn't seem to meet his eyes as they walked together to the elevator.

* * *

He took her to a quiet restaurant downtown, with white linen tablecloths and white candles on the tables, and a live string quartet playing chamber music. It was cozy, and intimate, and the food was exquisite. But she hardly tasted it. Her mind was whirling with questions. He seemed to sense her confusion as they lingered over a second cup of rich coffee. He set his cup down in the saucer abruptly and leaned back in his chair, studying her with a single-minded intensity that began to wear on her nerves.

"You're very lovely," he said without preamble.

"Thank you," she replied, and lifted her empty cup to her lips to give her nervous hands something to do.

He drew an ashtray closer and started to reach for his cigarettes when the waiter came back, and he paused long enough to order another cup of coffee for them before he finished the action.

"Men my age get used to a routine of sorts with women, Carla," he said gently, blowing out a cloud of gray smoke from his cigarette. "You disrupted mine."

"I...hadn't thought you'd expect that from me," she said falteringly. "Not so soon, at least," she added with a wistful smile. "I thought I'd have time to..."

"Don't start that again," he said. "I should have known what an innocent you are. All the signs were there, like banners. I was just too blind to see them. Anyway," he added with a brief smile, "there was no harm done."

"Wasn't there?" she asked, gazing quietly at the hard lines of his leonine face. They never semed to soften very much, she thought, even in passion—especially in passion. She flushed. "You were so angry," she recalled.

He chuckled softly. "Yes, I was. Hurting like hell, like I hadn't hurt since years before I married. I could have choked you to death. Not knowing the whole story, I thought you were playing hard-to-get. And to tell the truth, I hadn't planned to see you again.''

That hurt, more than she'd expected. Of course, most women her age were sophisticated and more permissive. But she'd been a late bloomer in all respects. Even now, when just looking at this dark, taciturn man could make her heart do flips, she couldn't consider an affair. She knew instinctively that it would tear her to pieces emotionally, especially when it ended. And it would end sometime. He was too sophisticated and far too worldly, to be satisfied with a novice for long.

''Why did you change your mind?'' she asked gently.

He lifted his coffee cup with a well-manicured hand. ''Because I missed you.'' A fleeting smile played around his chiseled lips. "It was unexpected. I've had women around since my wife died, but only briefly, and in one capacity. It occurred to me, belatedly, that I enjoyed having you around." He looked straight into her eyes. "In any capacity."

Her lips felt suddenly dry, and she moistened them with the tip of her tongue. "I couldn't handle an affair with you," she said hesitantly.

"I won't ask you to. But, if you don't mind, honey," he added with a wry smile, "I think we'll keep it low key. I can't handle frustration. It plays hell with my temper."

She smiled self-consciously, remembering. Her jade eyes looked into his. "I hope you know that I wasn't playing coy," she added seriously.

"I know it now." His dark eyes studied that portion of her above the table with a sensuous boldness that made her heart thump. "I'd say I wish I'd known it sooner, but I don't. I can still close my eyes and taste you.''

She felt the heat in her face. "Low key, I believe you said?" she said breathlessly.

"Honey, for me this *is* low key." He chuckled. "Finish your coffee, and we'll take in a movie before we go home. Do you like science fiction?"

"I love it!" she said incredulously. "Don't tell me you're a sci-fi fan, too?"

"Don't let it get around but I sat through two showings of *Star Wars*," he replied with a smile. "And if you aren't in a hurry for your beauty sleep, I'll sit you through two showings of this one."

"Who wants to sleep?" she asked, gulping down the rest of the rich coffee. "Why are you sitting there?" she asked, standing. "The box office opens again at nine!"

"Just give me a minute to ease my

aching old bones out of the chair,'' he chuckled, leaning forward to stamp out his cigarette.

''Shall I get you a cane?'' she asked with a mischievous smile. Her eyes traced his formidable bulk as he rose. ''Or maybe a forklift?'' she added, measuring him with her eyes.

''I'm not that big.''

''You're not small,'' she returned. ''I'll bet that's why you got elected.''

He scowled. ''What is?''

''Your size. The voters simply couldn't see your opponents when they were out campaigning against you.''

His leonine head lifted, and he stared down his straight nose at her through narrowed, glittering eyes. ''You,'' he said, ''are incorrigible.''

''Look who's calling who names,'' she replied saucily. ''You wrote the book on it.''

He smiled down at her, a slow, wicked smile that was echoed by the look in his eyes. "Has anyone ever told you that this kind of teasing raises a man's blood pressure at least ten points?"

She turned and started toward the cashier's counter. "I won't do it any more," she promised. "At your age, that could be extremely dangerous."

"Why, you little..."

"You're the one who was complaining about your age, not me," she reminded him.

"You make me feel it," he said with exasperation in his voice.

She waited patiently while he paid the check, her eyes drawn to an impressionistic study of ballerinas on a huge canvas on the wall. The delicate pink and white contrasts were exquisitely implied.

"Do you like ballet?" he asked at her shoulder.

"Very much," she replied, turning to follow him out onto the sidewalk. "I studied ballet for two years, until they convinced me that I simply didn't have the discipline to be good at it.''

"Discipline smooths the rough edges around any talent," he said with a sideways glance. "But I'd have said you have it, as far as reporting goes."

"Thank you," she said gravely. "I try to do my best. Although sometimes, it's easier than others. I could have gone through the ground that day I got into it with Edward King on your ghetto tour."

He raised a heavy eyebrow at her. "That wasn't the end of it, either," he informed her. "I got an earful when I walked into my office."

She flushed. "He was pretty mad, I guess," she probed.

"Putting it mildly, he was frothing at the mouth," he replied.

She drew in a weary breath. "I'm bound to do my job," she said quietly. "I still feel that Mr. King is being unnecessarily evasive about that land purchase, and I intend to pursue it until I get the truth.''

His jaw tautened. ''I think you're making a mountain out of a lump, little girl,'' he said flatly. ''Ed's like a mule. When someone tries to force him along, he balks. It's in his nature.''

''And not being put off is in mine,'' she returned with spirit. She stopped under a streetlight and stared up at him. ''Why can't I see the records of the land purchase?''

''I told you before, you'll have to knock that around with Ed. I'm not interfering,'' he said gruffly.

''Green says...'' She caught herself just in time. It wouldn't do to give away her hand, even though she was dying to know if Green's accusation about Moreland and King being such thick friends was true. And it was beginning to look bad; almost as if Moreland was involved, and had something to hide.

"Yes?" he said curtly, taking her up on the unfinished statement, his face like a thundercloud. "What does he say?"

She shrugged. "I'm sorry. Sometimes I forget to leave my job at the office."

He said nothing, leading her to the parked car in an ominous silence. "I'd better get you into the theater before we come to blows," he said, and she could hear the anger in his voice.

She felt a twinge of guilt, glancing at his set features as he climbed behind the wheel and started the black Jaguar.

"I'm sorry," she said gently.

Something in his posture relaxed. He pulled out into the traffic, all without looking at her. "Let's leave politics alone from now on. We both tend to overheat a little."

"All right," she agreed. She glanced

at him again, her eyes searching his dark face for some softening. There was none.

"I don't hold it against you that you're the mayor," she reminded him.

A hint of a smile flared briefly on his lips. "I'll trade jobs any time you like."

"No, thanks." Her eyes were drawn to his dark, beautiful hands as he controlled the powerful car with ease and skill. The onyx ring on his little finger sparkled in the sporadic streetlights. "Why did you want to be mayor, anyway?"

"Are we conducting an interview?" he mused.

"No," she said, "but I'm curious."

"I saw some things that needed to be done. They weren't being done. I thought I could do them," he said.

"And, have you?" she asked, genuinely curious, because her brief time in the city wasn't enough for her to know.

"Some of them," he admitted. "I'm bound by the city charter and the council. My hands are tied a good bit of the time."

"It looks like you'll get your redevelopment program through, though."

His face clouded in the dim light. "Maybe. It depends on my support."

He pulled into a vacant parking spot right in front of the theater.

"That never happens for me," she sighed wistfully.

He half-turned in his seat. "What?" he asked with a curious smile.

"A vacant parking spot where I want to go." She shook her head. "You must be incredibly lucky."

"I was, until I met you," he replied, tongue-in-cheek.

She saw what he was talking about and felt the color run into her face just as he got out to open the door for her.

The movie was a dud, one of its main features being a brief flash of bare flesh and some passionate love scenes that Carla found frankly embarrassing to watch in mixed company.

"You little puritan," he accused gently when the film was finally over and they were leaving the crowded lobby. "I could see you blushing even in the dark."

"I'm a country girl," she muttered.

"Come out to my farm in the spring, and let's see if you blush any less," he challenged dryly.

"Will you hush?" she burst out.

He laughed at her, a pleasant, deep sound. "I'd rather tease you than eat. Ready to go home, little one?"

No, she thought, watching him out of the corner of her eye as they walked down the sidewalk toward the car. I never want to leave you. The thought was incredible and she could barely believe what her stirred senses were telling her. She got a tight rein on her emotions, and slid gracefully into the car when he held the door open for her.

"I am a little tired," she admitted, forcing down her disappointment.

"I'll drop you by your apartment before I go home for my warm milk and crackers," he said dryly, sparing her an amused glance as he started the car and pulled out into the street.

"If you're drinking warm milk," she observed, "it's probably spiked."

He chuckled softly. "Probably."

They managed a companionable silence the rest of the way back to her apartment. It wasn't until they went up in the elevator that he broke it.

"Do you like to bowl?" he asked.

She laughed. "I like to try," she admitted. "Most of the time the ball goes down the alley."

"I'll teach you," he told her. "All it takes is the right technique and a little practice."

"I'd like that," she said, smiling up at him.

He searched her soft green eyes and scowled as they left the elevator and walked down the carpeted hall to her door.

"Is something wrong?" she asked, when they reached her apartment.

He rammed his hands in his pockets and sighed heavily. "Time," he said, sketching her face with restless eyes.

"Time?" she prompted.

"You need to be spending yours with a younger man," he said.

"I thought I was," she replied, darting a mischievous glance up at him.

He shook his head. "It's only a matter of time before someone mistakes me for your father."

"Only if I wear roller skates and braid my hair," she assured him.

He reached out a big hand and touched her cheek lightly. "Are you sure?" he asked.

Her face went solemn. "Am I too young for you?" she asked gently. "I know so little..."

"That makes you a novelty in my life," he replied. He pulled at a lock of her long, dark hair. "I know very little of innocence. My wife was far from being a novice when I married her. And I wouldn't have married her if Candy hadn't been on the way."

"What a lovely name," she murmured.

"She was a lovely little girl," he replied quietly. His dark eyes clouded.

Her fingers went up to touch his chiseled mouth. "You've never talked about it, have you? Not once. Not to anyone."

"You read me very well, little one," he told her, catching her soft fingers to press them against the hard lines of his cheek. "No, I haven't talked about it. But I think I could, with you."

"I'm flattered."

"It's not flattery." He drew her palm to his mouth, and she felt the warm excitement of his lips against its softness, running through her like electricity.

She could smell the clean, tangy scent of his skin as the action brought his dark head closer. She felt her heart storming against the walls of her chest. He affected her as no man ever had. Everything about him attracted her; the bigness of him, the dark masculinity, even the scent of his cologne. She wanted with all her might to reach up and bring that hard mouth down against her lips.

He looked up and saw the expression in her face, and something seemed to explode in his dark eyes.

"Don't tempt me, honey," he said in a soft, deep tone. "If I start kissing you right now, there won't be any stopping me."

She flushed. "I wasn't..." she protested weakly.

His dark eyes sparkled wickedly. "Weren't you?" he teased.

She lowered her eyes to the heavy rise and fall of his massive chest, hating her inherent shyness.

"Don't be embarrassed," he said gently, and she felt his fingers lightly touching her hair. "Delicious things happen when I touch you. You'll never know what it cost me to walk away from you that day at the farm."

She smiled at the carpet. "I felt terrible," she murmured. "I didn't sleep for two nights, and I was sure you hated me."

"You do inspire violent emotions, little one," he said wryly, "but hatred isn't one of them. Not for me." He sighed, leaning his forearms over her slender shoulders. "I knew you weren't sophisticated, but that innocence—I thought it was more a pose than anything else, and I indulged you. But the way you responded to me..."

She lowered her eyes to the steady rise and fall of his massive chest. ''I've got a mental block about sleeping with men,'' she admitted quietly. ''I believe in forever afters.''

''And probably, unicorns,'' he teased lightly. ''I'll be honest, Carla, I've tried marriage and I find little to recommend it. I enjoy my freedom.''

''And the women that go with it,'' she said with a wry glance.

He looked vaguely uncomfortable. ''Do you want to know something irritating, little girl? I haven't had a woman since the night of that cocktail party.''

She flushed at the frank statement. ''Lack of opportunity?'' she asked breathlessly.

''Lack of interest,'' he replied. His heavy brows drew together in a scowl. ''I want you. No one else.''

''Bryan, I'm sorry...''

He laughed mirthlessly. ''God deliver me from innocence," he said in a gruff undertone. "It may be gold floss to fiction writers, but it's hell on a man's appetite."

She felt her temper catching fire and abruptly she jerked away from him, opening her door. She stood just inside it, her pale green eyes flaring up as they met his puzzled glance.

"Let's just say good-night, and goodbye, and it's been fun," she said tightly. "I'm dreadfully sorry I leave a bad taste in your mouth, but I want more out of life than one night in a man's bed! Good night!"

She slammed the door and locked it, leaning her hot forehead against it tearfully, feeling its coolness drain some of the heat away. There was no sound outside in the hall for several seconds. Then there was a harsh, muffled curse and the sound of heavy footsteps dying away. Tears welled up and overflowed in her eyes, dribbling down her cheeks and into the corner of her mouth.

I hate him, she thought raggedly. Her eyes closed tightly. I hate him so much...

An ache made her chest feel hollow as the sobs wracked her slender body. A picture of his dark, handsome face floated around in her mind as she went to change clothes. It haunted her like an attractive, persistent ghost.

She did hate him—she did! Her even white teeth chewed on her lower lip as she stripped off the dress and exchanged it for a flowing gold and green patterned caftan. He didn't care a jot for her pale dreams of a home and children and a man to share with. He simply wanted her body—probably because it was the first that had been refused him.

The tears started again. She wiped them away with a vicious hand and went back into the living room. She didn't normally drink, but there was about two inches of wine in an old bottle in the cupboard, and she sloshed it into a juice glass and threw it down her throat. It stung pleasantly, giving her heartburn.

"Story of my life," she muttered, "cure's worse than the ailment."

She poured a glass of milk and washed the wine down with that, idly contemplating ways she could get even with Bryan Moreland. All of them seemed to end with her in his arms.

Her face went hot at the memory of the last time she'd been there, of a pleasure so intense it hurt. The touch of his hands, his mouth, the sight of his dark, quiet face above her with a strange glow in the orange firelight.

"Oh, God, I love you," she whispered shakily, her eyes closed as she saw him again and again in her mind. "I love you so."

The sound of her own voice sobered her, especially when she realized with a start what she'd been muttering. It shocked her so that she didn't hear the telephone until its third insistent ring.

Her heart jumped impatiently as she picked it up, hoping to hear Moreland's deep, slow voice on the other end. But it wasn't him. It was her informer.

"I just wanted to see what you'd come up with," Daniel Brown said lightly. "I hadn't heard anything from you lately."

"I'm still working on it," she said, aware in her heart that she hadn't really been working on it very hard. Part of her was terrified that Bryan Moreland just might be mixed up in the land deal.

"I know someone who can get you a copy of those financial records, if that's the impasse," he said. "By tomorrow morning, if you like. I could meet you in that little coffee shop on the mall."

"It wouldn't involve a break-in,

would it, Dan?'' she asked quickly. ''Our lawyers would frown...''

''I've got a girl friend at city hall,'' he interrupted. ''She'll do it for me. Well?''

She swallowed. ''I'd appreciate any help you could get me,'' she said finally. She was hurting so much from the confrontation with Moreland that very little of the conversation was registering in her mind.

''I hope you're not getting too involved with His Honor,'' he added suddenly. ''He's in it up to his thick neck, and I can get proof of that, too.''

Her face went white. ''What kind of proof?'' she asked in a voice far calmer than she felt inside.

''How about a check for one-hundred-thousand dollars, made out to him, signed by James White?'' he asked smugly.

She felt her heart stop, and for one long, insane instant she wondered if it would ever start again. "For what?" she managed.

"His share of the kickback, of course," Brown replied. "Moreland, White and King are all in it together. It was White's land. He had his agent, King, propose it to Moreland for the airport at a two-hundred percent profit, and Moreland buffaloed it over the City Council. It was worth about one-third of what the city paid for it, and one third is what the city got. The rest of it was split among the three men. White got the city's actual cost, plus a few thousand. The rest of it was split between Moreland and King. I'll bring you a photostat of the check, too."

She twisted the telephone cord round and round her finger. Her voice faltered when she found it. "I'll meet you at the coffee shop at ten-thirty."

"I'll be there."

Seven

She still didn't want to believe it. It didn't sound like Bryan Moreland. He had money—at least, she'd heard that he did, and the farm was big enough to be proof of some kind of independent wealth. And he had integrity. She'd have staked her life on his honesty, his forthrightness. Loving him had nothing to do with that opinion, either. She'd have felt that way if they'd been bitter enemies. She smiled to herself wistfully. After tonight, that might be the truth.

The doorbell sounded in the stillness, and she sighed wearily as she went to answer it. It was probably one of the neighbors....

She opened the door and looked up into a dark, quiet face with lines she hadn't seen before. He looked absolutely worn out.

"Got a cup of coffee?" he asked calmly.

She nodded, feeling her heart shaking her with its sudden, insistent pounding.

She stood back to let him in, pausing long enough to close the door before she led him into the kitchen and poured him a mug of fresh, hot coffee.

He leaned back against the counter to sip it, his dark eyes sliding up and down the caftan appraisingly. "You look very exotic in that," he remarked casually.

She shrugged. "It's kind of like walking around in a tent," she replied.

He smiled fleetingly, but the smile didn't reach his solemn eyes. Abruptly he set the cup down and reached for her, slamming her body against his, wrapping her up in his big, warm arms, holding her as though he was afraid she might vanish any second. His lips were against the side of her neck, pressing gently, softly.

She melted into him with a muffled sob, feeling the warmth and strength of his big body with a sense of wonder. Her arms stole inside his jacket and around him, her fingers tracing the hard, rippling muscles of his broad back.

"Damn you," he whispered in a searing undertone. "I haven't had a minute's peace since I met you."

"Neither have I," she said miserably. "Oh, go away, Bryan...!"

"I can't," he said, drawing back to look down at her with brooding, strange eyes. "You've cast a spell on me."

A little of her old audacity came back. "That's funny, you don't look like a toad."

"Don't be funny," he said, and his face was as hard, as formidable as ever. "I don't feel like laughing right now."

"What do you feel like?" she asked without thinking.

His eyes narrowed, glittering at her out of his leonine face. "Like picking you up and throwing you down on the nearest bed," he said harshly. "Not for one lousy night, but every night for the rest of my life."

She stared at him as if she wasn't sure she'd heard him. "What do you mean?" she asked softly, afraid of the answer even as she asked the question.

"Don't you know?" he laughed mockingly.

She dropped her gaze to his white shirt. "Bryan…"

He tipped her face up to his descending mouth, and it bit into hers before she could even begin to form a coherent thought. He was rough with her, as if he'd been holding back as long as he could, and his control was wearing thin.

"Open your mouth," he whispered unsteadily, roughly, his hand tangling in her long, loosened hair, as he pulled her head roughly back onto his shoulder. "Wide, Carla…" he said huskily, his arm crushing her, his kiss deepening intimately, blotting out thought, regret, sanity.

A moan broke from her throat, and he pulled away just enough to search her drowsy, confused eyes. "You see?" he asked in a voice that was deep and slow and not quite steady. "I could make you submit. I don't even have to work at it. I touch you, and your body flares up against mine like a torch.'' He brushed his open mouth against her forehead. ''You can talk about morality from now until hell freezes over, but if I pressed you, you'd let me have you, Carla. Not because of an uncontrollable desire, but beause you're in love with me.''

She felt the shock run through her body as if she'd touched a live wire. He knew! But how could he, when she'd only just discovered it herself?

He felt the sudden stiffening of her body in his arms and drew back to study her. ''Don't panic.''

She swallowed hard. It was unnerving to meet that level, intense gaze. ''I...I didn't realize...it showed,'' she said weakly.

''You have a very expressive face, little one. It was flashing like a neon sign tonight, even through that burst of temper.'' He locked his hands behind her back and swung her lazily back and forth. "I walked around the block twice, muttering to myself, until it suddenly occurred to me that the only reason you were so angry was because you wanted me as much as I wanted you." He smiled wryly. "Then it stood to reason that you cared too much for a casual fling, and all the puzzle pieces just fell into place. I came back to see if I was right."

The embarrassment was like a living thing. She felt weighed down by it. "I...it's still an impasse," she said quietly. "I know you could force me, but I'd hate you."

He shook his head. "You'd love me," he corrected. His eyes looked deep into hers. "It would be everything either of us could want, for the rest of our lives."

"But, desire isn't enough...." she protested weakly.

A corner of his chiseled mouth went

up. "Did I neglect to mention that I'm in love with you?"

Tears burned in her eyes, hot and overflowing down onto her flushed cheeks in a tiny flood. He blurred above her.

"Don't," he whispered. His fingers lightly brushed away the tears.

"It's like coming to life all over again," she murmured shakily, "after being dead inside. Sunlight..."

"I know." His lips brushed her wet eyes. "You taste of wine," he whispered at her mouth. "Trying to drink me out of your system?"

"Umhum," she murmured. She smiled wistfully. "It didn't work."

"Liquor won't do it," he whispered, kissing her softly, possessively. "But a few weeks behind closed doors might. We'll go on the way we have for a little while longer," he added seriously. "Until you're very sure. But I don't have a doubt in my mind how it's going to end.''

"Neither do I,'' she murmured. Her eyes studied the strong, hard lines of his face.

"What are you looking at?'' he asked.

"You never seem to really relax, to let go,'' she said gently. "I was wondering if you ever do, even with a woman.''

He smiled gently at the expression on her face. "Oh, I let go, all right,'' he laughed softly. "Would you like me to show you?''

She lowered her eyes shyly. "I think you'd better go home.''

"I think so, too.'' He studied the caftan. "I can't feel anything except skin under that flowing thing, and I'm getting ideas right and left.''

"I wasn't expecting company.''

"But you were hoping, weren't you?'' he asked perceptively.

"Yes," she admitted, her heart in her eyes. "Oh, yes, I was."

He stopped the words with his hard mouth, kissing her roughly, briefly. "Sleep well. Meet me at the office around twelve, and I'll take you to lunch."

She blanched, remembering her meeting with Brown, the accusations...but she put them all out of her mind for the time being. She smiled. "I'll be there."

She didn't sleep for a long time, thinking about the night that had ended so unexpectedly. It was hard to believe that a man like Bryan Moreland could actually be in love with her. She had so little; he had so much. But between them, they seemed to have everything.

Her mouth was still bruised from the pressure of his, her ribs still ached from the embrace that had seemed to crush her. A man couldn't pretend that kind of emotion, she thought dazedly. And to realize that a man she loved could feel that way in return amazed her.

Brown's words came back to haunt her, tearing the delicate fabric of her dreams. Tomorrow, she'd go to meet him, and maybe all his accusations would vanish like nightmares in the daylight. She wouldn't—she couldn't—believe what he'd told her. Bryan Moreland wasn't a crook; she was sure of that. She fell asleep finally, with a picture of Moreland's leonine face in her soft eyes.

Daniel Brown was waiting for her in the small coffee shop where she'd arranged to meet him, his long pale fingers nervously clutching the fragile stem of the half-empty wineglass that held what remained of a cup of coffee and a smear of whippped cream. He looked up as she entered, and a relieved expression crossed his face.

She forced a smile she didn't feel

and sat down in the chair he pulled out for her.

"Nippy out today, isn't it?" she asked, slipping out of her heavy black coat.

"A little." He took a quick sip of his coffee. "Can I order something for you?"

"Espresso," she said.

He gave the waitress her order and sat back down with a heavy sigh.

"Have you got it?" she asked suddenly. Better to have the truth all at once, if it was the truth, than to dig it out a sentence at a time.

But even as she hoped he might not be able to produce that damning evidence, he reached in his pocket and pushed a folded sheaf of photostat copies across the spotless white linen tablecloth at her.

With a hard swallow, she opened the papers with trembling fingers and looked at the first of the copies. Her heart felt suddenly like an anchor in her chest. Her green eyes closed momentarily. It was a check for one-hundred-thousand dollars, made out to Bryan Moreland, signed by James White. Her gaze flashed to Daniel Brown's curious, wary face.

"I know what you're thinking," he said unexpectedly. "Look at the second photostat before you say it."

Puzzled, she turned to the second sheet, and saw what he meant. This photostat was the endorsed back of the check, with Moreland's unmistakable signature.

Dully, she thumbed through the rest of the material. There was a photostat of a page of financial records with the disbursement of five-hundred-thousand dollars to James White Realty for a tract of land marked airport land purchase. Another sheet was from the tax assessors office, showing the fair market value of the property at one-hundred-thousand dollars. It was enough, more than enough, to give to the paper's legal staff. In fact, the very obvious overpayment might be enough to make an accusation and prosecute.

"This will destroy Bryan Moreland politically," she murmured.

"Probably," came the cool reply. "But the evidence speaks for itself. They were trying to cover up an overpayment of four-hundred thousand dollars—of which your aging boyfriend received one-fourth. Explain that, if you can."

She stared at him, pausing while the waitress put the cup of espresso in front of her. "Now tell me the real reason why you're doing this," she asked quietly.

He looked taken aback. "I told you already, I..."

Her eyes narrowed. "I know what you *told* me. I want the truth."

He shrugged, averting his gaze. "All

right, maybe I felt like a little revenge. We were in love, you know.''

"You and who?'' she persisted.

"Mrs. Moreland, of course,'' he said bitterly. ''She was much younger than he was, and he treated her like dirt. She was nuts about me.''

Those words haunted her all the way back to the office. Something wasn't quite right, although revenge might be a good motive for helping to nab a crook. But if it wasn't revenge...

When she handed over the photostats to Edwards, he and the legal staff were convinced that they had a blockbuster of a story.

"You've done a damned good job, Carla,'' Edwards told her with a rare smile. ''I knew you'd pull it off.''

"Brown won't testify, you know,'' she said. ''And I can't reveal my source by telling where and how I came by those photostats.''

"We'll work that out," he assured her.

"What if..." she cleared her throat. "What if it's a frame?"

He studied her closely. "You know better than to get involved with a news source."

She nodded, and smiled bitterly. "You can't imagine how well I've learned that lesson."

"Go eat something," he said with a paternal pat on her shoulder. "It will all come right."

Bill Peck stopped her just as she started out the newsroom door. "Want to have lunch with me and talk about it?" he asked with uncharacteristic kindness.

She shook her head. "Thanks. But there's something I've got to do first."

His eyes narrowed. "Don't go. He'll rip you into small pieces."

Her thin shoulders lifted fatalistically. "There's very little left to be ripped up," she said in an anguished tone. "See you."

She walked into the waiting room of Moreland's office with a heart that felt as if it had been pounded with a sledge hammer. Her face was pale, without its usual animation, and her body felt as taut as rawhide.

"Go right in, Miss Maxwell," his secretary said with a smile.

"Thank you," Carla said gently. She opened the door to his office with just a slight hesitation.

He was sitting behind the big desk, his dark eyes riveted to her trim figure dressed in a gray suit and black boots. A smile relaxed the hard lines in his face and made him seem younger, less intense.

"Sexy as hell," he remarked with gentle amusement.

She swallowed, and not to save her

life could she return his smile. "Hello,
Bryan," she said in a loud whisper.

The smile faded. "What's wrong?"
he asked gently. "Did you stop by to
tell me you couldn't make it for
lunch?"

Her shoulders lifted slightly, as she
gathered her courage. "I don't think
you're going to want to take me out
when you hear what I've come to say."

His heavy black brows collided. "Sit
down."

She shook her head. "If it's all the
same to you, I think I'll stand," she
said miserably. She fumbled in her
purse for the photostats she'd made of
Brown's material. "I think this will explain it all," she said, handing them to
him. She waited while he studied the
documents, his eyes narrowing, his face
becoming as hard, as formidable as she
remembered it from their first conflict.

His dark eyes flashed up to her face,

blazing. "Well?" he growled. "What about it?"

She curbed an impulse to turn and run. "Do I really have to tell you that?" she asked in as calm a voice as she could manage. "We're going to publish this information. We can't afford not to."

His jaw tautened. "You think this check is a kickback?" he asked in a strange, deep tone.

"We know it is," she agreed tightly. "It's painfully obvious that you don't pay five times fair market value for a piece of land unless somebody benefits. We've already checked with the man who owns the land. All he got out of the deal was two-hundred-fifty-thousand dollars. That leaves the other half unaccounted for, except for your cut. Either White alone or with another conspirator pocketed the rest, and we can prove it. I'm sorry, but..."

"You believe I'd take a kickback?"

he asked with barely controlled rage. "You really believe I'm capable of that kind of vice?"

"You accepted a check from James White for one-hundred-thousand dollars," she said in a voice that trembled, "just two days after the check for the airport land left city hall. What else am I supposed to think?"

"Get out."

He said it so softly, so calmly, that she did a double take. He didn't raise his voice, but then, he didn't have to. There was an arctic smoothness in his words.

She turned to go. "I'm sorry," she said inadequately, her voice a bare whisper. Inside, she felt as if she were frozen forever.

"Not half as sorry as you're going to be, I promise you," he said. "One more thing, Carla."

"What?"

"Was it really necessary to get that

involved with me to get the story?'' he asked coolly. ''Did you have to pretend an emotional interest, or was that just a whim?''

Her face reddened. ''But, it wasn't...''

He laughed shortly, leaning back in his chair to study her with eyes that shone with hatred. ''I should have been suspicious at the beginning,'' he said mockingly. ''A woman your age wouldn't have been so interested in a middle-aged man. I suppose I was too flattered to ask questions.''

''But, Bryan, you don't understand...!'' she cried.

He ignored her. His eyes were those of a stranger. ''Go print your story,'' he said. ''You might add a postscript. I got my funding for downtown revitalization this morning. I may leave this office, but I'll take the city slums with me.''

Tears blinded her. She turned and ran

out of the office leaving a puzzled secretary staring after her.

The story hit the stands the next afternoon, with a blazing banner headline that read, ''Kickback Suspected in Airport Land Purchase.'' The story carried Carla's byline, even though Edwards had had a hand in writing it. She hadn't slept the night before at all. She could imagine the anguish Moreland was going through. She'd destroyed him. And he thought that she'd been pretending when she said she loved him. That hurt most of all, that he could believe she'd be that cruel for the sake of a story. But, after all, didn't she believe that he'd been crooked enough to take a kickback? How could she blame him?

Over and over she heard his deep voice growling at her accusingly. It began to haunt her. And Daniel Brown's voice haunted her as well, admitting that he'd been in love with Mrs. Moreland, that she was "nuts about him." From what she'd heard about Angelica Moreland, she was hardly a lovable woman. And she would have had to be a good deal older than Brown, who was still in his middle twenties. None of it made sense. If only she could get her mind together enough to think logically!

She walked into the newsroom the next day with a feeling of unreality. Her mind was still on yesterday, but Peck snapped her out of it with his greeting.

"We're into it now," he greeted her grimly. "Moreland's filed suit for defamation and character assassination."

"Did you expect him to admit he was guilty?" she asked with a bitter smile.

He grinned back. "Hell, no." His pale brows drew together. "Something bothering you besides the obvious? Making accusations sometimes goes with the job, honey. Reporters don't win popularity contests, you know.''

"I know." She slumped in her chair. "What do you know about the late Mrs. Moreland?''

"Angelica?" He shrugged. "She liked men and money, and she hated her husband and motherhood. That about wraps it up.''

"What kind of men did she like? Young ones?''

"Angelica?!" he exclaimed. "My God, she liked them older than her husband. I think it must have been a father fixation. She was never seen with a man under fifty except Moreland.''

Her lips made a thin line. "Do you know anybody who could help me get some information on Daniel Brown's private life?''

One eyebrow went up and he grinned. "Think Moreland's innocent?''

Her chin lifted. "Yes." Her eyes dared him to make a comment.

He only smiled. "So do I." He laughed at her expression. "Don't look so surprised, honey. I've known His Honor for a lot of years, and he's got more integrity than any other public official I know. Sure, I'll help you dig out some info on Brown. I think he had an angle, too."

She returned the smile, feeling a weight lift off her shoulders. "Then, let's go. I want to see a man I know at the city police department about some personnel records."

"I'll check with a contact of mine," he said, following her out the door. "My God, don't we remind you of the news staff on that hit television show?"

She laughed. "Which one? The one where we solve crime and make America safe for consumers, or the one where we fight for truth, justice and the..."

"Never mind. Let's sneak out before Eddy can ask where we're going."

"I don't think he cares if we even work today," she replied. "He looked sick when I poked my head in to ask about assignments, and he didn't even offer me one."

"He's brooding over the lawsuit," he told her. "The attorneys warned him that he mightn't have enough concrete evidence to avoid one, but he took the chance. Without asking old man Johnson," he added, grimacing.

"He didn't ask the publisher?" she exclaimed.

He shrugged. "He couldn't reach him by phone, and the deadline was coming up fast. He took a gamble on the hottest story in years. Now Johnson's all over him like ants over honey."

She felt herself shrinking inside as she remembered whose byline the story carried. "How much trouble am I in?" she asked softly.

"I don't know," he replied, glancing at her sympathetically. "I wish I could tell you your job's secure, regardless. But I can't. That's the first thing Moreland's going to want by way of recompense if the evidence against him is false."

"Which I think it is," she murmured weakly. She stuck her hands in the pockets of her coat as they walked outside in the chill air. "It's going to be winter soon," she remarked, shivering.

He drew in a breath of cold air, unaware of the pollution judging by his expression. "What's that poem, 'keep spring within your heart, if winter comes, to warm the cold of disillusion...'"

"I didn't know you like poetry," she said, feeling the words with a sense of aching grief.

"An occasional line," he chuckled.

"Even though it goes against the grain. Come on, we'll catch a bus downtown."

"Lead on."

Carla, who was used to a two-man police department, couldn't help but be awed by the mammoth precinct with crowds of lawbreakers and blue uniforms and plainclothes detectives. She felt uncomfortable among all the unfamiliar faces.

"Don't worry," Peck assured her, "none of them bite."

"Care to lay odds?" she whispered.

"Shhh!" he said sharply. "Not here!"

She flushed at his teasing tone. "I wasn't trying to gamble with you," she protested.

"Discussing a capital crime, right in front of the city's finest!" he clucked. "Shame, shame."

"Will you stop," she muttered. "I'm a good girl, I am."

"So was Ma Barker."

"Why did we come here?"

"To see Leroy."

Her eyebrows went up, but he moved forward to haul a patrolman off to one side. There was a lot of whispering, and gesturing, and the tall, dark-haired, middle-aged policeman was giving Carla a look that made her feel vaguely undressed.

They joined her at the door, and Peck took her arm, propelling her out onto the street with Leroy right behind.

"We'll grab a cup of coffee and talk," Peck said, leading them toward a nearby cafe. "Carla Maxwell, Leroy Sample."

They exchanged mumbled pleasantries and walked along in a companionable silence. Once inside the old cafe, which featured worn, bare wood floors and vinyl-covered booths repaired with black electrical tape, they talked over strong coffee.

"What do you want to know about Daniel?" Leroy asked with a grin. "I don't know much, but I'll do my best."

"Is he local?" Peck asked, all reporter now, not the jovial companion of minutes ago.

"No," Leroy replied. "He came here from Florida about six months ago, and was he a ball of fire! He was going to clean up all the corruption in the city and close down drugs and gambling for good."

"And then..." Peck prodded.

"You want the truth?" Leroy asked, lowering his voice. "He was offered a little temptation to turn his head, and he turned it. Some of the rest of us have been made the same offer, but we nixed it. He liked the dough."

"You think somebody's paying him still, even though he's been fired?" Peck asked.

"We all know he was feeding you that bull on Moreland," the patrolman said angrily. "With all due respect, I hope he sues the hell out of you. If Moreland took money, he had a legitimate reason. He's not on the take. I'd know."

Carla felt her heart lift, and she prayed silently that this fierce policeman was right. "Who's paying Brown?" Peck asked point blank.

Leroy looked uncomfortable. "I do my job the best way I can, and I try hard not to stick my nose out too far. Those guys play rough, Peck. I've got a little girl three months old."

The reporter sighed. "You make me feel like a heel for asking. I know how dangerous it is. I've had my share of threats, too. Okay, if you can't tell me, send me to somebody who can."

Leroy sipped his coffee. "Now you make *me* feel like a heel."

"It isn't deliberate," Peck said with a smile.

The policeman took a deep breath and looked around at the sparsely peopled cafe. His eyes came back to Peck. "I'll deny it if you finger me as your informant."

Peck looked vaguely insulted. "Have you forgotten that I stood a thirty-day jail term two years ago when Judge Carter tried to get me to tell who gave me information in the Jones murder?" he asked.

Leroy laughed. "Yeah, I had. Sorry." He leaned forward on his forearms. "You go ask James White who helped him ramrod that land deal through the city council, and you'll get your man."

Eight

Carla and Bill Peck wore ruts in the city park as they walked. A rally protesting the low wages paid garbage collectors was going on around them, part of the sanitation strike plaguing the city, but they ignored the peaceful marchers.

"He's right," Peck said finally, turning to Carla under a leafless oak amid the crunch of dead leaves underfoot.

"The best defense in the world is a good offense. We may still be able to pull our acorns out of the fire."

She blinked at him. "I don't understand."

"We'll go to see James White. We'll carry along a file folder of documents incriminating him. We'll allow him to give his side of the story before we print the whole disgusting mess."

"But we don't have any incriminating documents!" she burst out.

"We will have," he grinned. "Come on. Time's a wasting. We may save your job yet, and Eddy's too."

"Let's go to it, then," she agreed, smiling as she hadn't felt like smiling for days. Maybe she could clear Moreland's name. That would make up for so much, even if he never forgave her for what she'd already done. If only she'd listened to her heart. If only she'd been suspicious of Daniel Brown's eager help. If only she hadn't been so de-

termined to get a scoop, to make Bill
Peck proud of her. She sighed as they
walked briskly back toward the newspaper office. Oh, if only...

The paper had already gone to bed
for the day when she and Peck left
again, armed with an impressive folder
of information. They still had not men-
tioned a word to Edwards whose face
was almost as long as his legs.

Carla had already called to make an
appointment with James White on the
pretext of purchasing some land. She
knew the foxy little man wouldn't be
eager to meet with the press, especially
after his honorable mention in the story
on Moreland.

They were ushered into his private
office by a young, buxom blond secretary whose smile was as empty as her
pale eyes.

White rose, gray haired and thin,
with astonishment plain in his pale face

when he suddenly recognized Bill Peck.

"Reporters!" he burst out. He glared at them. "Don't sit down," he warned, reaching for the telephone. "You won't be here long enough!"

Carla felt suddenly nervous and unsure of herself, but Bill Peck was not taken aback at all.

"Dial," he warned the older man, "and you'll be on the front page tomorrow afternoon."

White gazed at him warily, but he hesitated, his finger still on the dial.

"We came armed this time," Peck added, holding up the file folder. He smiled confidently. "I think you're going to want to cooperate, Mr. White. That way, you just may escape a long jail term."

White put down the receiver and laughed self-consciously. He whipped out a spotless handkerchief and wiped his perspiring brow. "Jail?" he said.

"Surely you're joking, Mr. Peck. I've done nothing illegal. In fact, the only crime I'm guilty of is getting my client better than fair market value for a piece of land."

"And crucifying a blameless public official in the process," Carla broke in, feeling her advantage. She moved forward, and Bill Peck sat down, letting her carry the ball. She took the file from Peck and lifted it in front of James White's nervous face. "It's all here, Mr. White. Everything. How you arranged a five-hundred percent profit out of that worthless land. How you set up Bryan Moreland, you and your co-conspirator, to take the blame for it by sending him a check for his revitalization project just in time to make it look like a kickback from the land deal. We know all about it. We even know," she added narrowly, "about Daniel Brown's role."

White sat down, suddenly looking

his age. He leaned back in his chair and wiped his mouth with the handkerchief. His spare frame seemed to slump wearily.

"I engineered it," he admitted quietly. "There's no sense in denying it any further."

Peck pulled out a pocket tape recorder and turned it on. "I'm recording, Mr. White," he advised the man, "and I think it would be in your best interests to give the truth."

"Why not?" White sighed. "I'm ruined now, anyway, you'll see to that. Yes, I engineered the airport land deal. I got Ed King to present it to the City Council and convince his friend Moreland that it was the best site available." He nodded at Carla's shocked face. "Moreland had so much on his mind with the sanitation strike and that downtown redevelopment scheme that he wasn't able to check into the site too closely, so he left it all up to Ed, whom he trusted.'' He laughed shortly. ''Bryan and I have been friends for a long time, he had no reason to distrust me or Ed. We had it made. We sold the land to the city for five times its true value. Then I had Daniel Brown start making noises about Moreland accepting a kickback, right after I sent my good friend a donation for his downtown redevelopment. It was flawless. Absolutely flawless. Until you people came along and started poking around,'' he added bitterly.

''Who actually owned the land, Mr. White?'' Carla asked.

''The deed says, Will Jackson,'' he replied.

''But isn't it actually owned by Daniel Brown?'' she persisted, smiling at White's shocked expression. ''Yes, I made some phone calls to Florida. Brown used Will Jackson as an alias when he purchased that land, at your instructions.''

"At Ed King's," White corrected gruffly. "Why the hell did I ever get mixed up with that little snip? If I'd handled it by myself..."

"If," Carla sighed, closing her eyes momentarily as a wave of unbearable grief and tiredness washed over her. She turned away as Bill Peck moved to call the police. It was too much, too soon. All her suspicions, all her digging, and it hadn't been enough to save Bryan Moreland from a public crucifixion. She'd finally gotten at the truth, and all it had cost her was the one man she could ever truly love. A single tear rolled down her cold cheek, trickling salty and warm into the corner of her mouth.

"It's great," Edwards laughed as Carla and Bill Peck played the tape for him and summarized White's arrest. "Just great! We'll scoop every paper in town with this, even the broadcast boys! We'll save face!''

Carla stared down at her black boots. ''You'll print everything, including how Moreland was set up?''

Edwards looked at her with a compassionate smile. ''Yes. And it might be enough to convince him to drop the lawsuit. We'll run another banner headline. 'Moreland Innocent of Kickback.' How's that?''

''Will it please you-know-who?'' Peck asked, tongue-in-cheek, gesturing toward the ceiling.

Edwards frowned. ''God?'' he asked.

''The publisher!'' Peck burst out.

''Oh, him.'' Edwards shrugged. ''Nothing ever has before. I'm not sure it will. But it may save my job, and Carla's.''

Peck grinned. ''I'll settle for that.''

But, it appeared, Bryan Moreland wouldn't. Edwards called Carla into his office two hours after the paper was on the streets, looking uncomfortable and vaguely ill.

"Sit down," he said gruffly.

She perched herself on the edge of her chair and sat up straight, her hands clenched in the lap of her burgundy plaid skirt. She could feel the ominous vibrations, like the growing chill of the weather.

"Get it over with," she murmured. "I hate suspense."

He jammed his hands in his pockets and studied his feet. "Moreland called me."

Her heart jerked, but she didn't let the emotions dancing inside her find expression in her face. "Oh?"

"He's willing to drop the lawsuit, especially in view of our efforts—your efforts—to clear his name. But I couldn't get across to him that it was your investigation that cleared him," he added apologetically. "When I men-tioned your name, he blew up." He sighed. "What it boils down to is this. He'll drop the lawsuit if I fire you. That's my only option." He shuffled angrily. "Johnson says if I don't fire you, we'll both get the boot."

She felt every drop of color draining out of her face, but she forced a smile to her lips. "I expected it, you know," she said gently. "I was looking for a job when I found this one."

"Yeah," he said curtly. His eyes studied the expression on her pale face. "I'm sorry as hell."

She shrugged. "It's been an experience. How long have I got to clean out my desk?"

He sighed bitterly. "Until quitting time. I'm giving you two weeks pay, maybe that'll get you through to another job."

She tried to mask her apprehension with a smile. "I'll be okay. If things get too tight, I can always go home to

Georgia,'' she reminded him. ''The editor of Dad's old paper would give me a job on the spot. All I have to do is ask.''

That, at least, was true. But how was she going to leave this city, and Bryan Moreland behind, when the picture of them would haunt her until she died? If only she could see him once more, touch him...

''I said, you might have a shot at the radio station,'' he repeated, interrupting her melancholy thoughts. ''I hear they're looking for a leg person.''

She smiled and rose, offering him her slender hand. ''Thanks, Eddy. I've enjoyed working here.''

''You're one hell of a reporter,'' he said with grudging praise. ''I hate to lose you. If it weren't for that damned lawsuit—the truth is, our budget won't stand it, and he's got every law in the books on his side.''

''It was my fault...''

"And mine," he said firmly. "Nobody held a gun on me and made me print it. The evidence was there. I didn't know it was engineered any more than you did. By the way," he added, "there's every indication that Ed King is going to be recalled even before his case comes up," he grinned. "That ought to make you feel a little better."

She returned the smile. "It does. See you around, Eddy."

Bill Peck sat, perched on the edge of his chair, watching Carla clean out her desk, an enigmatic expression on his face. He ignored the phone that was screaming insistently beside him.

"Where will you go?" he asked gruffly.

She shrugged. "Back to my apartment to wallow in self-pity."

He chuckled in spite of himself. "Hell, does anything get you down?"

"Crocodiles," she murmured as she put the last of her notepads into a brown bag with her other possessions. "I never go near swamps for that reason." She closed the bag and turned, her eyes soft as they met his. "Thanks for everything, my friend."

His face tightened. "Thanks for nothing," he grunted. "I helped cost you your job. If I'd interfered at the beginning…"

"I believe in fate," she interrupted. "Don't you?"

"Suppose I called Moreland, and told him the truth?" he asked quietly.

"No," she replied, turning to face him. "What happened between Bryan and me…it's nothing to do with anyone else," she finished weakly. "If he wants to think that it was all my fault, let him. I'll be gone soon, anyway."

"Gone where?" he asked.

She smiled. "Home. I've missed it."

"Not a whole hell of a lot," he replied doggedly, "Or you wouldn't have stayed this long."

"I've learned things here that I could never have learned in a small town," she reminded him. "And you've shown me the ropes. I'll never forget you."

"Don't get mushy," he growled, moving forward to perch himself on her desk. "When are you leaving?"

"I've got two weeks before I have to make a definite decision," she told him, grateful for her own foresight in keeping up her savings deposits. It would give her a little more leeway.

"Then you may stay in the city?" he probed.

She looked down at the brown bag, testing its weight and rough texture. "I don't know. I don't want to think about it right now. It's been a rough week."

"Yeah."

"Thank you for helping me do it," she said fervently.

"I like the guy," he said, and his

pale eyes smiled at her. "Keep in touch, okay?"

"Okay. If you hear of any openings around town, let me know."

"I'll keep both ears open." The smile went out of his eyes. "I've gotten used to you. I won't want to look at this damned desk for a week."

"Have Betty sit on it," she suggested with an impish grin.

"Two-ton Betty?" he groaned. "Who'll pay to replace it?"

"Definitely not me," she told him. She took one last look around the busy office, its rushing reporters and ringing telephones and editors calling over the din. "How quiet it is here," she sighed.

"Good thing you're leaving," he replied. "Working here has deafened you."

"Don't take any wooden tips," she cautioned.

"You, too."

She turned and walked out the door

into the lobby. The temptation to cast a farewell glance over her shoulder was strong, but she didn't yield to it. With her head high, she walked out onto the busy sidewalk and merged in with the crowd.

Not going to work was new to Carla. Since her eighteenth birthday, she'd had a job of some kind, even if it was only a summer one working for her father. But to see four walls day after day, no new faces, no people, was like slow torture. She kept the television on, but the soap operas were more than she could bear, and the radio got on her nerves after the second day.

There was too much time: time to regret her behavior, time to think about Bryan Moreland and his ultimatum that the paper fire her. How he must hate her. Not only had she betrayed him falsely, but he even thought her declaration of love was part of that betrayal, that she'd pretended affection for him solely to get a story.

She almost laughed at the thought. And he'd said that no normal woman would be interested in a middle-aged man. Didn't he realize how very attractive he was? How strong and charming and exciting he was to be with? Didn't he realize that she'd have loved him if he'd been totally gray and walked with a cane? Age didn't matter. Time didn't matter. She'd have given anything for just a few years with him—to love him, to bear his children, to grow old with him.

Tears blurred her eyes. The firing was a message, as surely as if he'd given it in person. He was telling her, in the most deliberate way possible, that he wanted her out of his city. And she had a feeling that if she approached any other news media for a job, the doors would all be closed.

* * *

It must have come as a tremendous shock to him, realizing that two of his most trusted friends had set him up as the scapegoat for their land deal. And to top it all off, to think that a girl reporter would lead him on and flatter his vanity just to get the goods on him...

"But it isn't true," she whispered tearfully. "Oh, Bryan, it isn't true!"

She dropped down onto the soft cushions of the sofa and cried like a lost child. It was the first time she'd yielded to tears since her firing, but it seemed to ease the hurt a little.

By the end of the week, she was regaining some of her former spirit. She'd already decided that her only course of action was going home, but she wanted to wait until her father returned. That would be just another three or four days, and she couldn't spend them sitting in the apartment staring at the walls. She became a sightseer, taking buses all around the sprawling city to visit the park, the museums, the historic landmarks. It was all new to her suddenly, as if she'd gone around blind as a reporter and was just now seeing the city without her blinders.

The days went by quickly, and on the very last one she found herself retracing her steps through the ghetto she'd visited with Bryan Moreland. The slums were already being bulldozed down now, and signs were going up heralding the construction of new, modern apartments for low-income groups. She couldn't help feeling a surge of pride for the man who'd fought so hard to bring this dream to fruition. If only she could tell him how very proud she was.

Her slender figure looked even thinner than usual in the gray suit she was wearing. A pale green scarf around her throat emphasized her green eyes, and the braided coil of dark hair seemed even darker against it. The black coat and boots she wore seemed to fit in with the darkness of her mood as she walked aimlessly back toward the downtown business district, her sad eyes on the dirty, cracked sidewalk. She felt so miserable, so lost and alone. Her chest lifted in an aching sigh and she didn't notice where she was going until she ran head-on into another pedestrian. Strong hands came up to grip her arms, and she looked up with an apology on her lips. Then her heart leapt inside her chest.

Bryan Moreland's dark, angry eyes were looking straight down into hers, and she couldn't even manage a weak greeting, the shock of seeing him was so great.

Nine

She stood there looking up at him like a slender statue, without life or breath or strength.

His face was hard, haggard, and she searched its leonine contours with a drowning hunger, lingering on the curve of his mouth, the darkness of his narrow eyes.

"Excuse me," she said finally, breathlessly, moving back as if the touch of his hands scorched her.

He let her go abruptly and pushed his big fists into the pockets of his beige overcoat. "I thought you were on your way out of town, Miss Maxwell," he said roughly.

She nodded. "I...I leave tomorrow," she managed. "The...uh, the slums... it's going to be quite a feat."

"My going away present to the voters," he remarked curtly. "I won't run for reelection."

She dropped her eyes, feeling cut to the quick. "It was all my fault," she mumbled. "Saying I'm sorry won't even scratch the surface, but I am, oh, God, I am," she whispered fervently.

He laughed shortly, without a trace of humor. "Chalk it up to experience, honey," he said sharply. "Maybe next time you'll be a little more cautious about your methods."

She glanced up at his set face

through her long, dark lashes. He looked as formidable as ever, only harder. Her heart almost burst at the sight of him.

"There won't be a next time," she said absently. "I...I'm not going back into journalism." She smiled wanly. "I hate the very idea of it, now."

He scowled. "Guilty conscience, Miss Maxwell?" he asked mockingly. "A little late, isn't it?"

Tears blurred him in her eyes. "Yes," she said in a whisper.

He drew in a deep, harsh breath. "Just for the record, you'd never have gotten me as far as the altar. I wanted you pretty damned bad, but one night would have worked you out of my system." His smile was cruel and mocking. "Too bad things worked out the way they did. Another date or two, and I'd have had you."

A strange sound broke from her lips. It was like the end of a dream. She'd cradled the thought that at least he'd cared for her once. But now, she didn't even have that. Not even that! He'd only…wanted her!

Without thinking, she turned and ran away from him, the crowd blurring in her tear-filled eyes as she tore through it, deaf to the sound of her name being called roughly behind her.

She elbowed through a crowd waiting for a city bus at the corner and darted out across the busy street, too overwrought to notice that the pedestrian light was red. She never saw the taxi that turned the corner and sped straight toward her. She was dimly aware of a horrible hoarse cry from the curb and a sickening thud that seemed to paralyze her all over. Then there was a strange cold darkness that she fell into, swallowing her up in its veiled cocoon.

The first conscious breath she drew was incredibly painful. She felt a strange tightness in her chest and her hand encountered bandages under the thin nightgown she was wearing.

She couldn't remember what had happened. She was only aware of crisp sheets, medicinal smells and metallic noises all around her.

Her eyes slid open lazily, thick from drugs. They widened as Bill Peck came into view at her bedside.

"God, you gave us a fright," he said heavily, rising with a weary smile to stand beside the bed and hold her hand.

"Have I...been here long?" she whispered.

"Two days," he replied. "Give or take a few hours."

"How bad am I?" she asked, wondering how she could even talk, she hurt so much. It felt as if every bone in her body was broken.

"You've got several fractures, three broken ribs, a concussion, and you're damned lucky the cab driver had lightning reflexes or you'd be dead,'' came a rough angry voice from the doorway.

She turned her head, groaning with the effort, and found Bryan Moreland standing there, dark and forbidding, and looking as if he hadn't slept in a week. His sports shirt was open at the neck, his hair was ruffled, and he was plainly irritated.

''Sorry to disappoint you,'' she whispered miserably.

Some unreadable expression flashed across his face. ''Who the hell said you have?'' he demanded.

Bill Peck let go of her hand with a grin. ''If you don't mind, honey, I'm going to get out of the line of fire. Get well, huh? And if you need anything, just call.''

''Thanks,'' she said weakly.

He winked at Moreland and closed the door gently behind him.

Carla turned her eyes back to the

wall, moaning softly with the pain. "What do you want now?" she asked wearily. "A leg?"

"I want you to get well."

She bit her lower lip to keep the tears at bay. "I want to go home," she said tearfully. "My father..."

"Is still on his cruise," he finished for her. "He sent a cable the first day you were in here. Peck and I went to your apartment to get some gowns for you, and it was waiting under the door."

"Oh." She felt the tears wind down her cheek. She was hurt and she wanted her father.

"You're coming with me," he said without preamble.

She turned on the bed, her eyes staring at him as he stood looking down at her, his dark face daring her to argue.

"I can't," she told him.

"Maybe not, but you're sure as hell coming," he said doggedly, his jaw going taut as he studied her young, bruised face. "Mrs. Brodie's going to live in for the duration, until I get you back on your feet."

Her lips trembled. "You don't owe me anything."

His face seemed to darken, harden. "You got hit because I upset you. I might as well have thrown you under the wheels myself."

She closed her eyes. Would she ever be free of guilt? She wondered miserably. First hers, now his. She didn't want to be on his conscience. And most of all, she didn't want to go home with him, to have to see him every day, knowing that he hated her, blamed her, that he was only salving his conscience by having her around.

"I don't want to go," she whispered.

He gave a harsh sigh. "I don't want you around any more than you want to come," he growled at her, "but there isn't much choice. You can't go home with no one to look after you, and I'm damned well not going to let you stay with Peck!''

''Why not?'' she asked sharply. ''He'd take care of me.''

''So will I,'' he said, his dark eyes unfathomable as they studied her thin form under the sheets.

Her eyes closed, and tears washed out from under her tight eyelids. ''Please don't make me go,'' she pleaded unsteadily. ''Haven't you punished me enough?''

There was a long silence, and when she looked at him, his back was turned. He was staring out the window blankly, his hands rammed into his pockets. ''It's only for a few days,'' he said tightly. ''Until you're back on your feet. We'll both grit our teeth and bear it. Then you can damned well go home and get out of my life.''

She turned her face back to the wall, hating him, hating what she felt every time she looked at him. It was going to be pure hell, and if there had been any way she could have talked her way out of it, she would have. But all the doors were locked behind her.

She studied the white fences and bare trees and chilly-looking Herefords as Bryan Moreland's sleek Jaguar wound up the farm road.

All her arguments hadn't prevailed against the brooding, irritable mayor. He simply silenced her with a hard look and went right ahead. Even Bill Peck wouldn't take her side against Moreland. It was as if every friend she had had deserted her. No one was willing to stand against Moreland.

Mrs. Brodie was waiting for them at the front door, smiling and sympathetic. She reminded Carla of a loving, kind aunt, standing there in her white starched apron.

''There, there, you poor little girl,

we'll soon have you back on your feet," she cooed, following along behind Moreland as he carried Carla down the hall into a spacious bedroom with a blue and white French provincial color scheme.

"I could have walked," she protested as he laid her down gently on the canopied bed.

He stared down into her eyes without rising, and she was aware that Mrs. Brodie had disappeared, calling something back about fetching Carla some hot chicken soup.

"And broken Mrs. Brodie's romantic heart?" he chided. His dark eyes searched her wan, bruised face. Reluctantly his hand moved up to tuck a strand of dark hair behind her ear. "You do look terrible, little girl," he said gently.

The kindness in his voice brought tears surging up behind her eyelids. "Don't," she whispered brokenly.

His face shuttered. Abruptly he rose from the bed and moved away. "Mrs. Brodie will bring you some soup, and I'll get your suitcases. You'll probably feel more comfortable in a gown."

She stared at him with her heart in her eyes. The tears spilled over onto her flushed cheeks just in time to catch Mrs. Brodie's attention as she came in with soup and coffee on a tray.

"Oh, poor dear," she murmured, setting the tray down on the bedside tale. "Does it hurt very much?"

Carla took the handkerchief she offered, and dabbed at her red eyes. "Terribly," she whispered, but she wasn't talking about physical pain.

"I'll get you some aspirin directly. Right now, you eat this soup." She placed the tray on the bed across Carla's slender hips. "Bless your heart, I'm so glad Mr. Moreland brought you to me. I wondered what was wrong, of course, but it isn't my place to pry.

He's just been so bitter lately, and the way he rides that big black stallion of his, it's a wonder he hasn't killed himself." She sighed, watching with maternal concern as Carla started sipping the delicious broth. "That dreadful King person. How could he do something so terrible to a man like Mr. Moreland?" She sighed, her ample bosom rising indignantly. "Pretending to be his friend, and all—can you imagine? Thank goodness someone took the time and trouble to get the truth."

"Amen," she breathed softly.

"It was your paper that did it, wasn't it?" Mrs. Brodie asked shrewdly.

She dropped her eyes to the spotless blue coverlet. "It was my paper that started it," she said miserably.

Mrs. Brodie patted her shoulder gently. "It all came right, dear. Don't worry."

Nothing had come right, but she only

smiled. "The soup is very good," she murmured.

And Mrs. Brodie beamed.

Moreland made a conspicuous effort to stay completely out of her way in the evenings. Naturally, his job kept him away in the daytime. But even when he came home, he found things to keep him busy. Farm business, paperwork, phone calls, anything, it seemed, to keep him away from Carla's bedside. Even Mrs. Brodie noticed it.

"Why, Miss Maxwell will get the impression that you don't want her here, Mr. Moreland," Mrs. Brodie teased gently one evening when he made a rare visit to Carla's room.

Carla, who was sitting wrapped up in her fleecy white robe in an armchair by the window, only glanced his way. One look at the formidable, dark face, was enough to tell her how little he wanted to be in the same room with her.

"Mr. Moreland is busy, I'm sure," Carla said with a gentle smile. "It was...very kind of him to let me come here to recuperate. I already feel I'm imposing, without his having to entertain me."

Moreland's eyes were flashing fire. "Don't let her stay up too late," he told Mrs. Brodie. He turned and went out the door, his face like stone.

"I just don't understand," Mrs. Brodie sighed.

Carla did, but she couldn't begin to explain it and she wasn't going to try.

A few days later, she dressed in her jeans and a pale green T-shirt that matched her eyes. It was an effort just to stand, but once she'd dragged a brush through her long, waving black hair and washed her face she felt a little more alive. The bruises on her flawless skin were beginning to fade a little, to a purplish yellow, but she didn't bother with makeup. What would be the use?

She couldn't attract Bryan Moreland again if she were the world's most beautiful woman. He hated her too much for that.

She made her way down the hall on unsteady legs, glad that Mrs. Brodie had driven into town to do the shopping. Being here on her own had given her some incentive to rush her recuperation. The sooner she was able to go home, the better. If only her father's arrival hadn't been delayed.

"What the hell do you think you're doing?" came a startled, deeply angry voice from the direction of the study.

She froze in her tracks, half turning as Moreland exploded out of his study into the hall. He was dressed casually, too, in worn jeans and a deep burgundy velour shirt that she recognized with a blush as the one he'd worn during her last brief visit here.

"I...I was just going to the kitchen," she said weakly.

He moved closer, towering over her. "You crazy child," he said in a soft, deep tone.

Her wounded eyes lifted to his, and he drew in a sharp breath.

"You shouldn't be on your feet this soon," he said, his hard mouth compressing into a thin line as he studied her thin figure in the tight jeans and top.

"The sooner, the better," she said quietly. "I have to go home."

"When you're able," he agreed. His eyes narrowed, glittered, on her face. "My God, little one, you look so thin. As if a breeze would blow you all the way home."

He clouded in her vision, and she averted her face from the concern she read briefly in his gaze. "Don't feel sorry for me," she said tightly.

"Is that how it sounded?" he asked. His lean fingers came out to close over her shoulders. "I've got a pot of coffee in the study, and a roaring fire. Come keep me company until Mrs. Brodie gets back. I don't want you staggering around alone.''

''I'm not drunk, you know,'' she whispered, unnerved by his closeness, the electrifying touch of his warm, caressing hands on the delicate bones of her upper arms.

He drew her imperceptibly closer, and she could feel his smoky, warm breath against her forehead, the bridge of her nose. ''Would you like to be?'' he asked in a bitter, brooding tone. ''Maybe it's what we both need. To get staggering drunk and hold a wake over the past.''

She pulled away from him before he could read the submission in her eyes. ''I...I would like some coffee,'' she agreed.

He hesitated for just an instant before he took her arm and guided her into the study.

She hadn't realized it was the same

room; she'd been too wrapped up in Moreland. But as she recognized the fireplace and the rug, her face went white, and she stood like an ice sculpture in the doorway, just staring at it. The pain of memory was in her eyes, her face, her whole posture. A muffled sob escaped from her tight throat as she remembered with vivid clarity the sight of the two of them lying in each other's arms on the soft rug, the feel of his big arms warming her, loving her.

"I can't," she said on a broken gasp, turning away. "Please I'd like to lie back down."

He caught her flushed face in his big hands and turned her shimmering eyes up to his. "Lie with me, then," he said in a soft, haunted tone. "Go back with me."

Tears ran down her cheeks as her hands pressed warmly against his chest. "We can't," she whispered achingly. Her eyes touched every line of his face.

"I ruined everything," she murmured bitterly. "I killed it."

"Did you?" He bent, his mouth touching her own lightly, teasingly, tasting the tears that had trickled down from her eyes.

"The story..." she whispered. Her eyes closed, as she savored the feel of him against her, the tangy scent of him—cologne mixed with soap.... "Bryan," she breathed as his lips touched and lifted against hers.

"We made love on that rug," he whispered deeply. "Do you remember?"

A sob broke from her throbbing throat. "Every second," she said without pretense. "The story...had nothing to do with it. I loved you...."

His open mouth caught hers, pressing her lips apart as he bent and lifted her completely off the floor, cradling her trembling body against him as if she were some gentle, fragile treasure.

"Don't talk," he whispered against her soft, yielding mouth as he carried her toward the fireplace. "Make love with me. We'll heal each other."

A sob was muffled under his hard, devouring mouth. Her warm arms clutched at him, holding him as he laid her gently on the rug and came down beside her.

"I love you," she whispered softly.

"I'm years too old for you," he murmured against her cheek, his lips maddeningly slow and enticing.

"I'll push your wheelchair," she gasped as his mouth burned against her throat. "I'll polish your crutches. Bryan...I want children with you...."

She moaned under the hard, uncontrolled passion of his mouth as it forced hers open and searched it with an unfamiliar intimacy that made her blood run hot. This kind of ardor was something she'd never experienced before; she stiffened in instinctive fear at first.

But his arms tightened, and his ardor became suddenly gentler, coaxing, and with a sigh, she gave herself over to him completely. She wouldn't fight anymore. Whatever he wanted. Anything. Everything. Her cool fingers moved under the hem of his soft burgundy shirt and ran over his firm, hair-covered chest with a sense of awe. It was so good to touch him, to savor the powerful masculinity that drew her like a magnet. She loved him so. If all he wanted was a mistress, even that didn't matter. She moaned, her fingers digging into his muscular flesh as the kiss deepened sensuously.

Abruptly he drew back and rolled away from her to lie breathing heavily, his hands under his head, one knee drawn up.

She turned her head on the rug, staring at him not comprehending. "Did I do something wrong?" she asked softly.

"Pour me a cup of coffee," he said roughly. "It's behind you, on the table."

She sat up, feeling vaguely rejected, and turned around to the coffee table. She poured coffee into the two china cups and added cream in his, remembering how he liked it. She lifted his and set it on the rug beside him, then turned back to get her own, grimacing with the movement.

"Now do you know why I stopped?" he asked, raising an eyebrow at her as he sat up and lifted his cup.

She stared at him, lost in the warm darkness of his eyes.

He chuckled softly. All the hard lines were gone from his face. He looked years younger, carefree—loving.

"Your ribs, darling," he said gently, as he sipped his hot coffee. "You aren't up to violent lovemaking yet."

The "yet" made her pulses go wild.

She stared down into her black coffee. "You don't...hate me?" she asked.

"Look at me, country mouse," he breathed.

She lifted her shimmering, soft eyes to his and caught her breath at the emotion she read in them.

"I love you to the furtherest corner of my soul," he said quietly. "I've never loved this deeply, this completely. But you were a baby, and I was afraid of you. I didn't think you were capable of feeling deeply at your age."

She felt the warm glow wash over her body like scented water, and she smiled at him. "And now?"

He chuckled deeply. "If you could have seen the look on your face when you walked in here...it told me everything. That you cared. That you'd been hurting the way I had. That you loved me. It was like waking out of a nightmare."

"I'm so sorry," she began.

He pressed a long forefinger against her lips. "It's over—forgotten." His finger traced her soft, pink mouth. "Kiss me."

She leaned forward and drew her lips against his slowly, teasingly. "Like that?" she whispered saucily.

He caught the back of her head and ground her mouth into his for a long moment, making her ache with the barely contained passion in his kiss. "More like that," he replied with a mocking smile when she drew back, blushing.

She dropped her eyes to her coffee. "Did you really want me here?"

"Are you out of your mind?" he asked conversationally. "It was all I could think about. I reasoned that if I could get you here, keep you here long enough, you might be able to forgive me."

Her eyes misted once again as she

looked at him. "For what?" she asked incredulously.

"For almost costing you your life," he said, and his face went rigid with remembrance. "Oh, God, when I saw that taxi heading for you..." He stopped and caught his breath deeply. "I prayed every step of the way until I got to you, and I swore that if you lived I'd make it all up to you somehow."

"But it was I who'd caused you so much pain," she countered.

"We hurt each other," he said, summing it up. "But that's over. I want you to live with me."

"Yes," she said quietly.

"Aren't you going to ask me about the terms?" he asked with a slow grin.

She shook her head.

"Unconditional surrender?" he probed.

She nodded with a smile.

He caught her hand and took it to his lips. "Marry me, then."

"You don't have to."

He gave her a measuring glance. "I thought you just said you wanted children with me?"

She blushed wildly. "Well..."

"Yes or no?"

She met his teasing eyes levelly. "Yes. A boy, and maybe another girl," she added gently, sensing his pain.

He nodded. "The farm will be a good place for them to grow up."

She clutched his hand as if all the past few minutes were a delicious dream she was afraid of losing. "Oh, I only wish my father was home so that I could tell him."

"He is, and I already have," he said.

She gaped at him, tugging her hand loose. "He is?" she burst out.

He nodded. "I called him. He was here for those first few critical hours until we were sure you were going to be all right. Then I persuaded him to pretend he was still on vacation so I could take you home with me."

"However did you get him to agree?" she asked, aghast.

He touched her cheek gently. "I told him I was in love with you, country mouse, and that I was reasonably certain you were in love with me."

Her eyes closed briefly. "Is it real, or am I just dreaming again?" she said, more poignantly than she knew.

He stood up, drawing her with him. His face was strained. "We'd better go call your father before I give in to the temptation to show you how real it is. Think how shocked Mrs. Brodie would be," he added wickedly.

She reached up and touched his cheek. "Are you sure?" she asked quietly. "I'm not worldly, and..."

"Hush." He brushed her mouth with his. "You're my priceless treasure, and I'll treat you like paper-thin glass. All right?"

She flushed and turned away from his mischievous smile. "I thought we were going to call Dad."

He drew her into his arms. "In just a minute," he agreed, bending his head. "I think it can wait that long, don't you?"

She went on tiptoe to meet him halfway, her warm smile disappearing under the slow, expert pressure of his mouth. Yes, the phone call could wait. Everything could wait. She closed her eyes and gave herself up to the one man in all the world whom she could love forever. In the back of her mind were the lines of a poem... "Keep spring within your heart, if winter comes, to warm the cold of disillusion." The winter approaching would find spring flowering in her soft eyes.

* * * * *

A brand-new adventure featuring California's
most talked-about family, The Coltons!

SWEET CHILD
OF MINE

by bestselling author
Jean Brashear

When Mayor Michael Longstreet and social worker
Suzanne Jorgensen both find themselves in need of a spouse, they
agree to a short-term marriage of convenience. But neither plans
on their "arrangement" heating up into an all-out, passionate affair!

Coming in February 2004.

THE COLTONS
FAMILY. PRIVILEGE. POWER.

Silhouette®

Where love comes alive™

Give in to the indulgence...
Enjoy the decadence...
Explore the passion...

**Indulge in eight delicious tales
spun by today's hottest authors during
the DECADENT ESCAPES promotion!**

Reading Between the Lines
by Vicki Lewis Thompson, a *New York Times* bestselling author
and a Kelly Ripa "Pick of the Week," and Leslie Kelly

Lip Service
by *USA TODAY* bestselling author Lori Foster and Julie Elizabeth Leto

Beyond Suspicion
by *USA TODAY* bestselling author Suzanne Forster and Julie Kenner

Strangers in Paradise
by top-selling authors Stephanie Bond and Joanne Rock

*Included in all four volumes—a free book offer and huge
travel discounts! Send away for a Preferred Member
Hotel Accommodation card that will entitle you to savings
of up to 50% at hotels worldwide.*

*Look for this decadent promotion at your favorite retail outlet.
See inside books for details.*

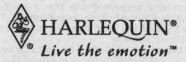

HARLEQUIN®
® *Live the emotion*™

Visit us at www.eHarlequin.com

NCPJAN04R

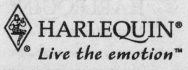

RCAD1